A Horse Called Trouble

D0107706

C.K. Volnek

Spark Books

A Horse Called Trouble
Copyright © 2011 by C.K. Volnek
First print edition
ISBN-13:978-0615572178 (Spark Books)

Cover design by
Spark Books
utilizing selected photo from
Kseniya Abramova/Photos.com

The Story

Abandoned at a young age, Tara Cummings has been passed from foster home to foster home; not wanted anywhere by anyone. At thirteen she's skeptic and suspicious, with no family, and no friends.

Horse therapy "will teach trust, perseverance, respect, and the value of teamwork," or so says the program's instructor. Tara is unconvinced. Trust only broke her heart, perseverance meant more failures, and no one respects or wants to team up with the misfit foster kid.

At the farm, Tara meets Trouble, an angry and defiant horse, bent on destroying everything and everyone around him. Tara is frightened of the enraged horse, until she realizes Trouble is as misunderstood and untrusting as she is. Pushing aside her fear, a special bond is formed, much to the surprise of everyone at the farm. Trouble trusts Tara, and Tara in turn finds hope and acceptance, as well as the will to love and trust again herself.

But, Tara's confidence is shaken as an even greater challenge looms ahead. Trouble's mean and manipulative owner is the one and only Alissa, Tara's nemesis. Can Tara overcome her own limitations and fight to save the horse who freed her heart and gave her life value and meaning? Or will Alissa destroy them both?

C.K. Volnek

ACKNOWLEDGMENTS

To Take Flight Farms, for allowing me to share in the extraordinary horse therapy program they provide...

To my sister, Amy, who was always there to share her passion of horses...

To my wonderful critique group, the Middle Critters, who helped make the horse Trouble come alive...

And, of course, to the many great horses I have loved for teaching me confidence, self-esteem, and trust...

Thank you.

CHAPTER ONE

The massive barn towered up into the Midwest sky, a prison of whitewashed boards, sunlight glinting off it. Might as well be barbed wire. Tara Cummings blinked, momentarily blinded.

So this was her punishment—horse therapy?

She shook her head, letting her mousy brown hair fall over her face. Another time she would have been thrilled to be here, to see a real horse, to actually touch one, not watch it on TV or the internet.

Her fingers tightened into a fist. This time was different. This was a sentence of shame—for something she hadn't even done. She didn't steal Alissa's purse!

Tara struggled to swallow the lump in her throat, the dryness in her mouth refusing to release the knot. Alissa had set her up—she was sure of it. She'd planted the purse in her locker. Why? What had she ever done? Because she wasn't cool...or popular...or wear designer clothes? Because she was a foster kid?

Resentment and desire burned as one in her chest. She'd *never* have money or popularity. She'd been born a have-not and the world was making sure she would always stay a have-not.

A cool morning breeze blew across the farmyard, cold fingers reminding the world that despite the sun and the absence of snow, it was only early spring and summer was still a long way off. Tara shivered and withdrew into her shabby sweatshirt, wrapping her skinny arms up in its scratchy fabric. She should have tried harder to prove her innocence to Principal Jackman. Should've made him listen.

A long breath whistled through her teeth. It wouldn't have made any difference. He wanted to be rid of her, like everyone else in her life. Teachers, foster parents, her own mother. All too happy to wash their hands and dump her onto someone else. No one cared. Why would Jackman be any different? He couldn't wait to ship her off to Marvel's, the east side's alternative to regular school. Marvel was, after all, the best place to dump all the 8th grade punks no one wanted.

Tara gazed from the barn to the crisp, white fences and luscious green pastures surrounding them. Marvel was known for its unusual methods in dealing with problem students. But she had totally not expected this. It had to be some kind of mistake. The other kids had moaned and groaned, certain they were headed for a work-camp, cleaning up horse crap, hauling hay, painting, and all that stuff. Listening to them, Tara had envisioned smelly, peeling barns, and broken-down fences. This was quite the opposite. The farm was actually quite tidy. Nice. Peaceful. Not the kind of place she'd expected juvies to be sent to at all.

Maybe this wouldn't be so bad after all.

A leaf rustled on the path in front of her, its dry brown contrasting against the spring-green grass. It twirled and danced on the gust of wind making its way from the barn toward Tara...along with the horrible stink. She pressed a ragged sleeve to her nose. Eww! It was everywhere. Like a subway toilet that

4

hadn't been flushed in weeks.

Who had she been kidding? This wasn't some nursery rhyme. Old McDonald's Farm. This was a place to be disciplined and chastised. She pressed her sleeve hard against her nose. Her classmates were right—they just wanted to make them clean up the stinky horse crap.

A horse screamed. A flock of sparrows took flight from the tree next to the barn, swirling into the air, a dark cloud of feathers chattering their irritation. Tara searched for the animal and jumped as it screamed again.

"Whoa," a man's voice bellowed from inside the gaping doorway. "Blast it, I said, *whoa!*"

A short, thick-necked man stumbled out, heels digging into the hard dirt as he fought to hold onto the red horse dancing in circles around him. He clung to the thick reins with one hand and pulled a leather whip from his rear pocket with the other, snapping it at the horse with a loud *crack*.

The horse laid his ears flat, flashed a mouthful of large teeth and dove at his captor, hatred sparking in his eyes. Stumbling backward, the man let loose of the reins, surprise and fear flooding his face.

Tara gasped, a small, barely audible squeak coming from her mouth.

The horse spun around to face her, ears swiveling, black hooves stamping and pawing at the ground. Rage flared his black nostrils.

Tara froze, a scream stuck in her throat, staring wide-eyed at the red horse.

"Get back, Miss," a voice ordered from behind her. Rough hands shoved her to the side of the path and a dark-haired man rushed forward, grabbing at the horse's reins. The horse reared, lashing out, black mane rippling like a nest of angry snakes. The dark-haired man held on.

5

blared again, his eyes wild, white rings
lack.

away as quick as she could, unable to take her
zed horse. Her heart pounded in her ears. She
wanted to get away. She *needed* to get away from this wild animal.
Staring into the horse's eyes, she couldn't move. There was
something…something in his eyes. She understood his look of
pain.

"Are you crazy, Richard?" the black-haired man yelled,
glancing back at Tara before turning his sole attention to the
horse. "You know we aren't supposed to have him on this side
of the barns today. Beth's therapy class is here." He glared at the
fancy leather saddle on the horse's back. "And, what's this
dressage crap doing on him again?"

Richard stepped back toward the barn door, his face a mix
of stubborn anger and impatience.

"I had my orders, Sam," Richard grunted. "Miss Jordan
called and told me to saddle him up. She wants to ride him."

Tara blinked. Jordan? Alissa Jordan? Here? The hair on the
back of her neck prickled. Her stomach rolled, the acidic taste of
bile rising to her throat. She forced it back down. It *had* to be a
different Jordan.

Sam pulled the horse down the path away from Tara,
moving to avoid the dangerous hooves. "No way is *anyone* riding
him, especially not in this get-up. He's *not* ready. And this stunt is
going to set him back even further."

Richard snorted. "Don't know why you're wasting your time
on this stupid animal anyway." He extracted a dirty handkerchief
from his pocket and wiped his glistening brow. "That horse
ought to be shot. The only thing he's good for is dog food."

Sam stopped and stared back at Richard, anger darkening his
eyes, his face turning almost as red as the horse. "I think you
better mind your chores, Richard, before I do something I might

regret—like tell Mr. McDonald you've been slacking on those stalls." With a loud grunt, he directed the rearing horse toward a small corral between the two barns. "Let *me* take care of this horse," he yelled over his shoulder.

Richard stuffed his handkerchief back in his rear pocket, the end sticking out like a grimy plaid tail. "You wait 'til Miss Jordan gets here," he scowled. "Then we'll see who 'takes care' of that horse."

Turning, Richard spotted Tara. He narrowed his eyes and growled to himself. "Slackers. Beth's asking for trouble bringing these punk kids here."

Tara shoulders tightened, anger biting at her tongue. Slacker? She wanted to scream, tell him, and everyone there, that wasn't her. She blinked hard and retreated under her hair, letting her shoulders slump. What good would it do? Everyone assumed she was trouble because of who she was—because of who her mother was. And even though she may not *be* trouble, trouble always seemed to find her.

Richard pushed the open barn door closed, revealing a large wheelbarrow filled to overflowing with filthy dirty straw. A black cloud of flies hummed around it like bees to honey.

Tara gagged and covered her nose and mouth again with her sleeve.

With a loud grunt, Richard boosted the wheelbarrow's handles and drove the smelly refuse down a winding path, disappearing behind a large shed at the bottom of the hill.

Finally, with Richard and the wheelbarrow gone, she dared to take a breath, coughing at the leftover stink, wishing she was somewhere else...anywhere but here. She didn't belong here.

Rejection bit at her. She didn't belong anywhere.

The big red horse screamed again, jolting her from her thoughts, forcing her to look up. Sam stood close to the horse in the corral and wrestled to maintain his hold with one hand while sweeping the saddle off with the other. With a flick of his hand, he slipped the bridle off and the horse was free. The red beast bolted away, hurtling around the fence, bucking and twisting.

Tara couldn't help but watch the horse, sadness drenching her like a cold rain. What had caused this animal to be so wild and crazy? Was this Miss Jordan as evil as the Alissa she knew? She couldn't blame the horse if that was the case.

Tara shuddered, a surge of sadness and anger rolling through her like an ocean wave. She knew how it felt to be at the brunt of such nastiness.

The horse slowed to an anxious prance, knees popping, black feet barely touching the ground. Tara watched, hypnotized by the curve of his neck, the spirited arch in his tail, the slender black legs, his sweat-darkened hide glistening in the sunlight. He was beautiful. How could Richard think he was only good for dog food?

Sam stood on the board fence, sad eyes watching the horse circle. With a sudden burst of speed, the red demon charged past the fence and kicked. Sam jumped off the board rail as a black hoof connected with the fence, a loud crack resonating throughout the yard.

Loud voices hooted behind Tara. Lowering her head, she peered out through her veil of hair at her fellow classmates. Six students, making up a school of misfits, though Tara knew she was the biggest misfit of all.

CHAPTER TWO

Tara chewed on her thumbnail, a silent plea repeating in her head as she watched her fellow classmates march up the path. Keep going. Don't stop.

Simone and Brandy leaned against each other, covering their noses at the lingering smell of the wheelbarrow. Philly and Jon tagged along behind them, their faces screwed-up, gagging and waving their hands. Brandy had been there the longest, going on over a year, transferred to Marvel's for drinking and smoking, or so Tara had overheard. Simone was different. She just hated school, and while hanging with the "wrong group of kids" (as Simone's mother had apparently called them), began skipping classes for weeks at a time. Her mom had insisted something be done with her.

"I tell you, it's slave labor," Jon groaned, his dyed blond Mohawk quivering as he leaned against Philly. "Bet they make *us* clean all this smelly crap up. It's so bogus."

Jon's story was similar to Brandy, though he came from the north side of the city.

Philly nodded and hitched up his wide-legged jeans. Within seconds, his jeans slipped back down his skinny behind, red plaid boxers puffing out.

With a thankful sigh, Tara's shoulders relaxed as they passed without so much as a glance in her direction. She really wasn't surprised though. She'd learned to be real good at being invisible.

A pair of size thirteen tennis shoes swaggered up next to her, loud retching noises spilling from the owner's mouth. "Oh man, Tara, you stink. Don't you ever wash your pits?"

Philly and Jon stopped and looked back, grinning and pointing.

Tara's cheeks rushed with heat. Yeah, she was invisible…to everyone except Clancy. She held her breath, willing the ground to open up and swallow her. No, wouldn't happen. Luck never played on her side.

Keeping her head down, she peered at the owner of the shoes from the corner of her eye. Clancy's long hair slithered over the collar of his large leather jacket, his face smug, mouth a leering grin. Tingling shivers crept up her back and she crossed her arms tightly across her chest, lowered her eyes, and hoped he hadn't seen her looking at him.

Clancy enjoyed being cruel. He'd said he got kicked out of his school because of his mouth. Tara had no problem believing him. He was pushy and arrogant and he ruled Marvel. Made it clear her first day when she'd accidentally sat in "his" chair. Things had gone from bad to worse for Tara. She hadn't meant to embarrass him when he dumped her out of his chair. She hadn't meant to smack him, especially not *there*. No guy likes to get hit *there*. Clancy had doubled over, squealing like a little girl, and a ripple of laughter surged through the classroom. Tara had never seen anyone so mad, though as soon as Clancy got back to his feet, his glower shushed the entire room. Tara shivered. She'd managed to stay out of his way for two weeks, remaining invisible—until now.

"Aww, you not gonna talk to me now? You think you're better than me?" Clancy jeered, his voice getting louder. "Can you believe her, Jon? Thinks she's better'n me?"

Tara closed her eyes, counting her heartbeats. He was waiting for a response. Probably wanting her to say something…anything to give him a reason to pound her here and now. She wouldn't. She couldn't. She'd keep her mouth shut, like always, and hope he'd get bored and leave her alone.

Something hard struck her temple, jerking her head sideways. Pain seared through her brain as tears swelled behind her eyes.

Clancy shrugged his shoulders, flipping his jacket collar up. Dark eyes darted back and forth, surveying the yard. Tara knew he was checking for the teacher, who was sure *not* to be around at the moment. Clancy excelled at finding the opportune times to torture her.

With a satisfied smirk, he lowered his arm and unsnapped the punk leather wrist-band on his arm, slipping it into his pocket before anyone could see it. Sunlight glinted off the pyramid-shaped studs as though mocking Tara along with the headache it had just given her.

Tara grated her teeth and curled her fingers, her fingernails biting into her palm. He was such a jerk. She wanted to pummel him with her fists. Wanted to stomp his feet till his toes bled.

Clancy caught her glare and narrowed his eyes, daring her to act out her anger.

With a stuttered heartbeat, Tara looked away, too afraid to move, too angry to speak. No, she wouldn't *do* anything.

Clancy leaned in close, his voice low and threatening. "Watch yourself, freak. No one makes a fool out of me twice."

Tara choked on his cigarette breath, the foul taste coating her tongue. Shoving her hands in her pockets to hide their shaking, she faded as far under her curtain of hair as she could. She shouldn't have looked at him. Stupid. Stupid. Stupid!

Clancy stomped off after the other students, his torture complete—for the moment. He joined Philly and Jon and pointed a thumb back at her. "What a wuss."

Her shoulders drooped forward, her stomach aching. Clancy was right. She was a wuss. Always letting people push her around. What was she supposed to do? Push back? If she did, she'd only get pushed down twice as hard.

She turned away from the students and gazed out over the rolling hills and rows of leafy trees lining the fences. Green pastures flowed, peaceful waves of an emerald ocean, blue sky vaulting above. A breeze rushed through the trees lining the road to the farm, rustling the spring leaves. She'd imagined this when she was little, pretending she was Laura Ingalls from the old *Little House on the Prairie* videos she'd found in the dumpster. They didn't have a VCR, but Grandma Kay had always welcomed her across the hall after her mom had passed out for the night, the smell of booze and smoke thick in their apartment.

Tara sighed. Life on the prairie seemed heavenly. But she'd never known anything except the city. And she'd never get away from it, either. Stuck, like a goldfish in a dirty fish tank at the dumpy pet store down the street. Doomed to the city's hard concrete sidewalks, dirty brick apartment buildings, choking exhaust fumes, and weeks' worth of reeking garbage.

Her vision blurred and she blinked back the wetness. "Maybe I'll run away," she muttered to herself. "Wouldn't that bust June's bubble? No more free government money for this foster kid?"

She hung her head. No, she didn't have the guts to run away either.

Miss Elizabeth marched toward the students at the barn door, notebook in hand. "Okay class. Thanks for waiting while I parked the van."

"Sure thing, Miss E," Clancy quipped and winked at Jon. "Anything to make our teach happy."

Miss Elizabeth frowned at Clancy. With a shake of her head she turned to the other students, pointing at each as she marked in her notebook. Her pen stopped momentarily, seemingly stuck on the page and she looked up, searching. Catching sight of Tara, she snapped her fingers and motioned to the group. Tara lowered her head and obediently moved toward the back of the group.

Miss Elizabeth pulled a black wallet from her jacket pocket. "Phillip, you left this on the car seat."

Philly bristled and grabbed the wallet. "It's Philly. Philly." He threw his hands up in the air and turned around, his white T-shirt billowing, showing the plaid boxers again. He spit on the ground.

A twinge of jealously stabbed at Tara. Philly had only been at the school for three days, sent there by his parents "to clean up his act." The other kids accepted him as if he'd always been there. She was never that lucky.

"Okay, okay," Miss Elizabeth snapped. "Philly. But, you will keep your tone civil with me." She pushed her chin-length hair behind her ear and cleared her throat. "Now, I expect you all to mind your manners today. This program is a big part of your grade this quarter. If you want to return to your conventional schools in the fall as ninth graders, you'll do as Robin tells you." Finished, she turned and led the students toward the barn entrance.

The thought of returning to the regular school made Tara shudder. Returning would only put her back in the same school with Alissa. Back to hell. Though here she was stuck with Clancy, which was almost as bad.

Lifting her gaze, her eyes connected with Clancy's. He

glowered at her, his lip curled into a half-snarl. She shrank back, letting the group tromp off ahead of her.

As she waited, her skin prickled. Someone was watching her, she could feel it. And it wasn't Clancy this time. Nervously, she scoured the yard. The red horse stood in the corral, still as a statue, head high, black eyes drilling into her.

Tara stared back. For a moment, she could feel something pass between them. He understood what she was going through, telling her not to let them push her around. With a snort, he spun around and bolted around the pen, bucking and kicking.

Breaking from her trance, Tara rolled her eyes. *He is a horse. A wild, crazy horse.*

A sad smile rose to her lips. He *was* wild and crazy. And he was going to fight them 'til he dropped. He wasn't going to take their crap.

Her smile faded, an ache burning deep in the pit of her stomach. Why couldn't she fight? Why couldn't she be strong and defiant? The smirking face of Alissa popped into her head. She was one reason. Tara could never win against her.

The horse slowed to a proud trot, swishing his tail, long mane flowing.

"Stay strong, horse," Tara whispered. "For both of us."

CHAPTER THREE

"Tara," Miss Elizabeth barked from inside the barn door. "Quit daydreaming and stay with the group."

Tara lowered her head and stumbled toward the barn entrance.

"Good morning." A red-haired woman smiled at the group, hands on her hips. "Welcome to Freedom Farms. My name is Robin Daniels and I'll be your equine instructor for the next nine Tuesdays. Here, you will be challenged to work hard, to discover and define what success means to you."

Clancy leaned into Jon and Philly, whispering, pointing at Tara.

Jon grinned and nodded, his eyes drilling into the front of Tara's sweatshirt. "Yeah, flat as road kill."

Tara hunched her shoulders and backed into the shadows behind Simone and Brandy. Why couldn't she be as invisible to Clancy as she was to everyone else? The others barely noticed her as long as she didn't give them a reason to. Why couldn't Clancy forget her first day?

Robin nodded toward the horses in the pastures. "Shortly you will meet the true teachers of our program, our horses. They will teach you many life skills, including trust, perseverance, and respect."

Tara rolled her eyes. Trust and respect—in this group? Like that was ever going to happen. She'd learned a long time ago she couldn't trust anyone. And there was no such thing as respect, not for her anyway.

"You will learn the value of teamwork to get what you want," Robin continued.

Tara shook her head. Teamwork wouldn't happen either. She couldn't even get picked for a stupid dodgeball team in PE last year. Nobody wanted her on their team.

She glanced at Clancy. He was still locked in tight with Jon and Philly, continuing to point at her and laugh—a hard laugh, sharper than the edge of a razor blade.

Nobody would pick her. Not unless there was something in it for them, make her do all the work. She eyed Clancy. Was that his plan?

"Now, let's get you geared up." Robin motioned for the students to follow her. "There are boots and helmets for everyone in the staff break-room."

Tara shuffled down the dusty aisle after the others, the hems of her thrift-store jeans trailing in the dirt. Boots and helmets? Where were the brooms and pitchforks?

The group followed Robin into a dingy room in the middle of the barn. A paint-chipped table, surrounded by mismatched chairs, stood at one end. Two benches and a set of metal lockers sat against the wall next to a huge canvas duffle bag, overflowing with an array of boots. A tub nearby contained a number of hard plastic helmets.

Clancy and Philly converged on the bag as Jon, Simone, and Brandy dug into the tub, tossing boots and helmets between them. Tara waited, fidgeting with a loose string on the back of a leather chair. Jon plopped into a chair across from her and flipped his tennis shoe at her, laughed, and pushed his foot into a brown boot. Soon, tennis shoes littered the floor and the students were making their way back out of the room, the sounds of their heavy heels stomping from the wood floor to the dirt aisle.

"Hurry up, Tara," Miss Elizabeth called from the door. "We don't have all day."

Tara slogged her way to the sagging bag. Disgust tugged at her lips as she pulled out a pair of manure-caked cowboy boots. She slipped them on, stomping her heel on the floor to force her complaining toes in. Grabbing the last remaining helmet, she placed it on her head and buckled it in place. It pitched unsteadily and tipped sideways.

"Let me help you," a woman said from a doorway on the opposite side of the room. A pleasant smile crossed her tanned face.

Tara turned to see who the woman was talking to. No one there. Looking back to the woman, fear and uncertainty flowed like ice in her veins. The last time anyone had made a definite effort to talk to her, she'd ended up face first on the cafeteria floor. She'd wanted to believe Alissa then. But she'd only pretended to be her friend, instead laying the trap for Mitch to trip her, covering her in ketchup, mustard, and syrup. The echo of the entire school lunchroom laughing pounded in her memory.

The woman's smile faded, a puzzled look filling her eyes.

It's fine," Tara mumbled, reaching up and slipping the helmet off without unbuckling it. With a small shake of her head, she let her hair fall, hoping it would allow her to disappear.

The blonde stepped forward, her ponytail swaying. "You won't need this for the first lesson, anyway. I'll tighten up the clasps and it'll be good to go when you need it. Okay?" She took the helmet and tucked it under her arm.

Tara stood silent, unsure how to respond.

"Whatever," she finally managed to say and made her way down the corridor, fighting the urge to look back. Nobody helped her. Not even her own mother. She'd ditched her without so much as a good-bye.

Tara's lip trembled. In her mind she saw the faded blue curtains and peeling wallpaper in her bedroom. She felt the icy wind blowing through the cracked window next to her bed. Her mother swayed in the doorway, ranting and raving, arms flailing. Tara cowered in the corner, shivering with fear and cold, clinging to her third grade math book. The skinny woman screeched louder and louder, beer slopping from the open can in one hand, ashes tumbling from the lit cigarette in her other.

"Where are my cig'rettes?"

"You didn't give me any money, Momma."

Her mother took a deep drag off the smoke between her nicotine-stained fingers and blew out a gray cloud. "Money? You stupid or something? I told you to put 'em under your coat. I showed you?"

"Grandma Kay said it's wrong to steal," Tara cried softly.

Her mother scowled, blood-shot eyes livid. "Grandma Kay? Stupid old cow. She's not your grandma."

The words stabbed at Tara's heart. No, Grandma Kay wasn't her real grandmother, but she loved her as if she was. Grandma Kay made her cookies. Grandma Kay played cards with her. Gave her a place to stay until her mom came home. She could count on Grandma Kay.

"I'm your mother! That old biddy was nobody." She steadied herself against the doorframe with one hand, a sneer crossing her gaunt face. "And now she's dead."

Tears welled in Tara's eyes.

Her mother's eyes narrowed. With the glowing cigarette in her mouth, she staggered to the bedside table and grabbed a white ceramic horse from the stained wood top. "And what's this piece of trash doing in my house?"

Tara wanted to run and grab the horse from her mother's hands, to rescue it one more time. She'd found it, dirty and broken, in a trashcan behind the apartments. It had taken hours to scrub it clean and glue its legs back on.

Her mother heaved the horse through the air, the figurine crashing into the wall above her. Tara ducked and curled into a ball as the shattered pieces pelted her head and arms.

"Like always, I have to do everythin' 'round here." Her mother spun around and stumbled toward the door. "I'll get my own cigarettes…Little Miss Goody Two-shoes,"

Tara stifled a sob.

"And maybe I'll jus' keep goin'. I've had enough!" Her mother slammed the front door behind her, the paper-thin apartment walls shuddering.

That was five Christmases ago. Tara could still see the apartment, its dirty walls and cracked ceilings. She'd tried hiding the fact her mother had left, but when the landlord came looking for his rent and found no money, he'd called the cops. Without anyone to take care of her, Tara was forced into foster care. Shuffled from home to home to home, she felt as unwanted and shattered as her ceramic horse.

"Tara," Miss Elizabeth snapped. "Pay attention. This way."

Tara stopped and turned around. All eyes were on her. Snickers rippled. A burning rush rose to her face.

Miss Elizabeth pointed to each of the students. "Simone, you partner up with Brandy."

Tara couldn't breathe. Not Clancy. Not Clancy.

"Jon, you and Philly."

No! Tara peered at Clancy. He eyed her like a hawk watching

a mouse. She inched backward, not daring to breath. Was this how a mouse felt, before he was devoured?

Miss Elizabeth made a check on the paper in her hands. "Clancy, you team up with Tara."

Tara shivered. This was definitely not good.

CHAPTER FOUR

Tara trailed after the others, her insides twisting. How could Miss Elizabeth team her up with Clancy? Couldn't anyone see what he had in mind? Tara let out the long breath she'd been holding, watching her feet stir up the dust on the dirt lane. A hand gripped her arm, pulling it behind her back and pinching it hard. A hiss in her ear forced her to swallow the scream in her throat as she was pushed to her knees. Between the pain of Clancy's hold and choking on his over-ripe armpits, she was ready to pass out, fuzzy blackness rimming her vision.

"Listen, freak," he growled into her ear. "You're gonna do what I tell you to in there. And you better not screw it up. You do and you'll regret the day you were born."

She squeezed her eyes tight. What did she have to do? She'd *gladly* do it and get it over with if he'd only leave her alone.

Clancy loosened his grip and wrenched her back to her feet. She jerked out of his hold and stood on the side of the path, rubbing her shoulder, glancing around for Miss Elizabeth. Why didn't she do something?

Tara looked up, searching. Miss Elizabeth was out of sight, disappeared around the curve of the trail with Robin and the girls. She hadn't seen it. Tara sighed. Of course. Clancy wouldn't dare get caught. He'd timed it just right.

Cradling her arm, she stepped off to the side of the road, letting Clancy move on ahead. It was probably for the best anyway. She was in enough trouble with him already. It would only make things worse for her if *he* got in trouble.

Clancy sauntered up to his friends. Tara stayed as far behind as possible, watching him. As far as she could without getting in trouble.

So what was the class supposed to do out here? Surly they didn't expect them to pick up horse poop out here! The blonde woman had mentioned a lesson. What kind of lesson were they to learn out here?

Robin held open a gate and once all the students were in the pasture and the gate secured, she returned to the front of the group. Holding up three sets of jumbled ropes with odd-looking straps branching off from silver rings, snaps, and buckles, she began to speak. "I have a halter and lead rope for each group. Your first lesson today is to catch a horse."

Catch a horse?

Tara wasn't the only one surprised. Gasps broke out from the others and Philly and Clancy gaped at each other before turning to stare at the small herd of horses on the other side of the pasture. The horses stared back.

Robin handed a halter and lead to Simone.

Simone twisted it over and over. "How does this thing work?"

"That's for you to figure out." Robin smiled.

Tara huddled in her sweatshirt. The horses seemed calm enough, at least right now. A shiver rippled down her back. What if they went ballistic, like the red horse back at the barn? She was supposed to walk up and catch a raving mad animal? This was insane!

As if reading her mind, Robin continued, "The horses we use in our program are quite gentle and tame. This won't be without challenge, though. You will work in pairs. Catch them in whatever manner you can. I'll be watching from here."

Tara still wasn't convinced. Besides, what in the world was catching a horse supposed to teach them?

Robin handed Clancy a halter and lead strap and pointed to a gray horse with a black mane and tail in the corner of the pasture. "You and your partner will catch Homer."

Tara studied the gray. The horse gazed back at the group, ears flicking, tail swishing up over his swayed back.

Robin grinned. "And don't let his 'old' horse appearance fool you. He's a prankster."

Clancy sniffed at the dirty lead rope in his hand and wrinkled his nose. "What am I supposed to do with this?" He held the snake-like rope away from his body, and with a look of disgust, threw it at Tara. "This should be familiar to you. Didn't your momma keep you on a leash? Woof. Woof."

Tara jumped, but not quick enough. The ropes smacked her thighs and fell at her feet. She rubbed at her stinging legs, tears stinging her eyes. She swiped them away before Clancy could see, unsure if they were from the pain or the mere mention of her mother. A burning filled her, a yearning for the family life she would never know.

"Clancy, you *will* be courteous to your partner," Miss Elizabeth corrected. "She is your teammate."

Tara gaped at her teacher. Finally, Miss Elizabeth was saying something?

Clancy nodded, pushing his long hair aside, giving her his best innocent smile. As soon as she turned, he accepted a high-five from Jon. Tilting his head, he scrutinized the horse and muttered to Tara. "Well, this should be easy enough. It's one stupid nag catching another. Even *you* can't screw it up."

Clancy stomped toward the horse. Homer watched him, head hanging midway between his shoulders and the ground. Without warning, he gave a small buck and trotted to the opposite corner of the pasture, head high, his black mane streaming in the air.

With a flick of his long tail, he dropped his head to graze again. Tara grinned, a slight warmth radiating inside. Homer wasn't going to make this as easy as Clancy thought.

Turning back to the halter and lead, she twisted the strange-looking straps over and over in her hand. Unbuckling the clasp, she imagined how it would fit over the horse's head.

Clancy stormed across the pasture toward Homer's new spot, cursing under his breath, the sides of his jacket billowing in the breeze. "Come on, Tara," he yelled. "Get that stupid nag."

Homer peeked at Clancy from around his hindquarters and pranced off once again.

Tara struggled to keep from laughing out loud. She marveled at the ease of Homer's stride, his knees high, tail floating behind him like a banner. He reminded her of Traveller, General Lee's gallant horse. She'd done her history report on him last year.

Homer tossed his head playfully, stopped, and lowered his head to graze on the thin blades of new grass.

Clancy thrust his hands up in the air, shaking his fists. "Stupid horse." His face reddened to a deep crimson as he watched the other students. Jon and Philly had already captured their black horse and now stood arguing with each other how to put the halter on. Brandy and Simone had cornered their horse and seemed to be closing in.

Clancy turned sharply to Tara and pointed to Homer. "You better catch him this time, Tara. Or else…"

Tara slunk away, hoping her obedience would give Clancy a

reason to cool off. She angled toward Homer, shifting the halter in her hands. Homer lifted his head as she approached, watching her, a gleam in his eye, both curious and mischievous. Tara stopped. Such beautiful brown eyes.

Out of the corner of her eye, Tara caught Clancy circling behind the horse. He crouched, arms stretched, like a big cat stalking its prey. She tensed, willing him to stop.

Too late.

Homer snapped to attention, head high, snorting.

"Clancy, you goon," she whispered through gritted teeth, making sure her voice couldn't be heard by anyone other than herself. "You're going to scare him off again."

The horse gave a small buck and galloped away from Clancy, directly at Tara. Clancy ran after him, arms waving, yelling, "Get him, Tara!"

"Clancy!" Robin called from the top of the hill. "Don't…"

Tara's eyes widened as Homer hurtled toward her, large feet thundering. Catch him? Was Clancy kidding?

With a jerk, she threw the halter and lead rope at Homer, praying it would stop him or at least scare him in another direction. It didn't.

She spun around and raced down the slope. In one instant she was running, in the next, her boot tangling in the dense grass. Down she fell, flat, with a thud, her breath smashed from her lungs. Struggling to recapture her breath, the hoof beats pounded ever closer. The earth shuddered. There was no time to escape.

Tara closed her eyes and rolled into a ball, covering her head with her arms, bracing for what was to come. The sound of galloping thundered in her ears, louder and louder…until, holding her breath, she realized the pounding was her own heart. The hoof beats had stopped. A loud snort rumbled near her ear and hot breath warmed the back of her neck. She had escaped the horse's hooves. Was she now to be ripped apart by his huge horse teeth?

Homer whickered low, blowing into her hair. Tara sat up, slow and wary, and turned to find herself face to face with Homer's nose. He grunted and pulled at her hair with his big lips, his long whiskers tickling the side of her face. A grin spread across her face and she giggled.

"Tara, you idiot!" Clancy bellowed. "Why'd you throw the rope? Now, how are we going to catch him?"

Tara hid her face behind Homer's head. It wouldn't be good to have Clancy catch her smiling. Didn't matter if it was the horse's fault or not.

Homer snatched a mouthful of grass next to her foot, shaking a fly away from his ear. As she watched, he stopped chewing and stared into her eyes. Seconds seemed to last for hours, until Homer began chewing again, nudging her with his nose, grunting. If Tara didn't know better, she'd swear he was laughing.

"Maybe you don't want to be caught, huh?" she asked Homer in a low voice. "Maybe you want to do the catching."

Clancy cursed and kicked at the ground, a dirt clod zinging down the hill.

Tara stood and stepped closer to Homer. He continued to graze, biting off bits of long grass with loud munching sounds. She reached out, and then hesitated. Would he let her pet him? She reached again, her fingers shaking.

Homer continued to graze as Tara's fingers made contact with his dappled neck. It was silky-smooth and oh so warm. Her fingers slid down his long neck and his skin quivered. She yanked her arm back, bracing, sure he was ready to take flight. Homer kept on chewing. A fly buzzed up and over his head. Again, Tara reached, stroking his shoulder, her fingers gliding over his sleek hide.

She rolled the coarse strands of black mane between her

fingers. Homer raised his head, a soft sparkle glimmering in his dark eyes. She touched his velvety nose, smiling as his warm breath bathed her hand. He whickered softly, gazing at her, her image reflected in his eyes. Tara frowned at the sight. A pale face and sad eyes peered through a veil of messy hair.

"Oh, that's just great!" Clancy roared again, pointing to the other end of the pasture. "Everyone's caught their horse but us!"

Homer snorted at the outburst, laying his ears back and swishing his tail threateningly.

"We don't care, do we boy?" Tara whispered as she stroked Homer's face, watching Simone and Brandy proudly lead their red roan horse up to Robin, the rope wrapped around the horse's neck, halter flopping loosely under the horse's head.

Tara grinned, raising an eyebrow. "I guess that's one way to catch a horse."

Homer whickered again, seeming to agree with her. Leaning in, she wrapped her arms around his neck. "Does this count as 'caught'?" She sighed and breathed in the horsey smell. This was even better than any of her horse dreams. Homer was so…alive.

"Time's up," Robin called. "Clancy, come on back. Cindy will put the halter on Homer for you and get him to the barn."

Tara stayed in position, her arms around the horse's neck. His warm body seemed to melt into her and she had no desire to move. The grass rustled behind her. Metal clinked as someone readied the halter and lifted it to Homer's head.

"Okay, we've got him now," a woman's voice said.

Tara turned to see the blonde who had helped her with the helmet.

"He can be so naughty, can't he?" The woman patted Homer's shoulder and playfully tugged at his forelock. "He likes to tease. But you'll love him once you get to know him. We all do." She smiled at Tara. "I'm Cindy."

Tara nodded, her tongue mute.

Cindy handed her the lead and continued, "Why don't you take him up to the gate? I'll be right there. I need to check one of the other horses before we head in and get ready for the next lesson." She turned and strolled down the hill and up to a leggy brown horse.

Tara watched her go. Suspicion toyed with her, digging sharp talons into her stomach and driving twinges up and down her spine. The last time an adult had been this nice to her for no reason was when creepy old Mr. Wagner, the junkyard owner, had offered her five bucks for a kiss. She'd almost accepted, her growling belly driving her toward the round, sweaty man, toward the tobacco-stained smile, a leering glint in his eye. At the last second, her brain took over, pushing her hunger back, and she jumped back, out of reach of the grimy hands so close to trapping her in his wicked snare.

Confusion clouded Tara's mind as she blinked the rancid memory away. What could Cindy want from her?

CHAPTER FIVE

Tara jumped as the coarse rope came to life in her hand, the lead tugging at her fingers. A ripple of fear shot up her arm, her body tensing, ready to drop the rope if Homer tried to run for it. He didn't. He merely grunted and lowered his head, rubbing his ear against his leg.

She grabbed the lead with both hands, her fingers stiff, feeling chiseled of stone. Something inside took over and she tugged lightly at the lead, joy fluttering in her chest as the big gray followed obediently. The others would probably think this was only a trivial feat. To her it was monumental…to have something so big and strong follow her, to do as she asked. She turned around to lead Homer toward the gate.

Clancy leaned against the fence, face red, arms crossed tightly across his chest.

Tara's mouth went dry, a clammy cold gripping her stomach, fumbling with the lead rope in her hand. Why did he still have to be here?

"You moron," he snarled, his voice low and biting. "I can't

believe what a screw-up you are. And you're nuts if you think you're going to be the one showing up at the barn with that nag. Give him here." Clancy reached forward, jerking Homer's rope from her hands.

Homer snorted and snapped his head back, a glare of resistance filling his once placid eyes.

"Whoa, there, Homer." Cindy's voice was low and calming as she moved quietly along the other side of the horse. She put one hand on Homer's nose and firmly took the lead from Clancy with the other. "Homer doesn't like to be man-handled," she stated, a definite edge in her tone. "He'll put on the brakes if he thinks you're trying to jerk him around. Watch his body language and you can tell."

Clancy's jaw twitched and he coughed, throwing his hands up in mock surrender. "Didn't mean to. Guess I'm stronger than I realize."

"Well, *I'll* take him back to the barn," Cindy said, a polite yet tight smile on her face. "Why don't you join your friends?" She motioned to Philly and Jon as they trailed the volunteer leading their black horse.

Clancy glowered at Tara, and with a reluctant grunt, jogged off to catch up with the boys. Tara's shoulders relaxed. She was safe, for the moment. Heaven only knew for how long though. The grip on her stomach constricted again. Clancy was sure to get her good once they were back at the barn.

Cindy led Homer toward the barn. Tara followed. Despite her wariness, self-preservation urged her to stay close to Cindy. Homer's black tail swayed back and forth with each step and soon Tara fell into step with his steady gait. He was a powerful, huge animal, yet she felt safe with him. A grin crept to the corners of her mouth. Maybe she hadn't caught Homer the way Clancy thought she should have. She had caught him, her way.

At the barn, Cindy paused, leaning in and talking quietly with

Robin. Without looking back she continued on, her ponytail swaying in rhythm with Homer's tail. Tara wondered what the next lesson could be. What could possibly top catching a horse?

Clancy sat on a bale of straw outside one of the stalls. He stood as they neared and the clammy hold grabbed Tara's throat.

"Clancy," Robin called from the front of the barn. "Will you help the other two boys with their horse for the remainder of the class today? They could use the extra hand. Cindy will help Tara with Homer."

The surprise hit Tara like a brick. Thankful? Yes she was most thankful. Had Cindy done this for her? But how had Cindy known?

Clancy's shoulders stiffened as he glowered at Tara, and then rolling his eyes, he shrugged. "Yeah. Whatever."

Clancy rambled down the aisle toward Philly and Jon, spouting his smack. Relief flowed through Tara. Maybe this would give him time to cool off, or better yet, give her a chance to figure out how to stay out of his way. She still didn't understand why Cindy had done it? What was in it for her?

Dust flew into the air with each step of Homer's large hooves. Tara watched the particles, dancing in the shafts of light streaming through the window. Sickly-sweet aromas drifted from a small room off the main passageway, the smells mixing with soap and sweaty horseflesh.

Turning Homer around in the middle of the aisle, Cindy grabbed a lead strap hanging on the wall and snapped it to his halter. Reaching to a second lead on the opposite wall, she clipped it to his halter as well, securing him in a cross-tie position in the center of the aisle. Homer raised his head toward Tara and whickered, his large eyes sparkling as he reached his long nose toward her.

Cindy laughed. "I think you've got an admirer. I've never seen him take such a fancy to anyone so fast. He usually plays hard-to-get."

Tara hesitated. Glancing at Homer, she smiled and held her hand out. Homer rolled his big horsy lips over her palm, his breath warm and comforting. She moved closer, stroking his silky neck. She wasn't sure why, she felt safe with Homer, especially now, not having Clancy hovering over her.

She peeked at Cindy. "Thanks." Her voice was small. She swallowed, pushing herself to go on. "You know, for what you did back there with Clancy and all."

"For what?" Cindy grinned and winked. She nodded to a bucket next to the stall door. "Our next lesson is to teach you how to care for the horses. I'll show you how to brush Homer and take care of his feet."

Large, flat-bristled brushes stuck up out of the black bucket. Tara pulled an oval plastic-backed one out and handed it to Cindy. She slid the bristles against Homer's hide, brushing his shoulders with short, quick strokes, popping dust and dirt out of his coat and dragging the loose hair sideways.

Voices sifted through the barn. Three stalls down, Simone and Brandy bantered, tossing the brush back and forth with disgust, before popping out of Brandy's hand and rolling between their horse's stomping feet. Four more stalls farther, the boys leaned against the barn wall, watching disinterestedly as their volunteer demonstrated how to comb cockleburs out of their horse's mane.

"Here, you try," Cindy said, offering the brush to Tara.

She took the brush and pressed it against Homer's side, pulling it down his neck and shoulder. It slid easily, like ice on a hot tin slide. She stroked again and again as Cindy had shown her. Homer closed his eyes, stretched his neck and grunted, long and low.

Tara jerked her arms back, staring at the gray. Had she hurt him?

Cindy laughed lightly. "You've found the spot."

Tara swiped at her hair, pushing it out of her face. "What?"

Homer let out one last snotty breath.

"That's Homer's way of telling you he likes it. He's happy," Cindy said. "He likes you." She patted his rump affectionately. "Silly old horse."

Tara looked back to Homer. He liked her? She smiled. He didn't even know her and he liked her. Not even Mrs. Evan's big brown guinea pig had accepted her that fast. Even though she'd tried to be extremely careful, the normally placid little beast still took a chunk out of her finger.

Tara floated through the remainder of the lesson. Her shoulders relaxed as she brushed Homer's neck, sides, legs, and rump, cleaning his gray coat to a shimmer. He accepted the attention by hanging his head to doze. A feeling of contentment flowed up her arms, through her body, and down to her toes. She found herself standing straighter, taller—confidence filling her as Cindy complimented her on how well she was doing. She sailed through the lesson on how to put the saddle and bridle on, positioning the metal bit in Homer's mouth without so much as a slobber and cinching the small English saddle with ease. The others struggled to keep their horses still long enough to even set the saddle on the horses' backs.

Tara leaned into Homer and whispered, "Guess we make a good team, huh Homer?"

Team. Had she really said that? She'd never been part of a team. However, Homer made it so easy.

She pushed her hair behind her ears and breathed in. The smells she'd found so disgusting earlier were growing on her. Earthy smells. Horse smells. She hugged Homer's neck, feeling the silky warmth against her cheek, wishing she could stay here forever.

* * * *

As the school van sped down the highway, Tara leaned back and smiled, eyes closed, replaying the morning over and over in her mind. She could still smell the sweet grain mix of corn and oats in the feed bucket. She could feel Homer's sleek hide, silky soft under her hand. His breath was warm sunshine against her skin. Her heart skipped a beat as she thought back to Cindy's last comment…"You've really got a way with horses."

"What are you grinning at dork?" Clancy kicked her shoe, knocking it into the side of the vehicle.

Miss Elizabeth frowned from the rear-view mirror. "Tara, please don't kick the van."

"Yeah, Tara." Clancy laughed and made a face at her.

Tara turned to stare out the window. Yeah, Clancy loved getting her into trouble and then pretend he was so innocent. She knew she shouldn't let him get to her but he was such a jerk. Yet she dared not let him see how she felt. Especially not now. She was in enough trouble with him the way it was.

The city blocks rushed by as the van rolled toward school. How different Freedom Farms was from the concrete world she had always known. The farm was lush, green, and beautiful. The city was dirty and ugly. Grime-covered windows glared at her. Smelly garbage filled the dumpsters and gutters outside the apartments and restaurants. What *did* grow in the city seemed choked and stunted by exhaust fumes and cement sidewalks.

The van maneuvered past a small park. The memory of the corner park where she played when she lived with her mother sprang into her thoughts—a park with one rusty slide and two broken swings. The little bit of grass there was filled with dog poop and litter. Despite the garbage and smell, she had snuck there night after night to sit in the shadow of the slide and stare at the dark heavens, wishing upon the few tiny stars she could see above the city lights. Wishing her mother would change, wishing she could find the father she never knew and have a real family, wishing for a home where she was accepted and loved.

She jolted back to the present. What good did wishing do? Her mother had left. She had no home. And her father? He didn't even want to know her. He disappeared before she'd ever been born. Off to a life with the rodeo as a rodeo clown, Mom had said.

Tara's chest tightened. Why couldn't anyone love her? Really love her?

Her thoughts turned to Homer. Even though it had only been one class, she adored him. And he adored her back. She smiled, and glanced to make sure Clancy hadn't noticed her moment of joy. She closed her eyes, reliving the fresh air and green pastures. For the first time in her life she felt she belonged somewhere.

She frowned and leaned her head against the window, a hollow pain punching her in the stomach. Who was she kidding? She didn't belong anywhere.

CHAPTER SIX

Tara stared at the clock in the classroom. The seconds ticked endlessly. Time was dragging. She put her head on her desk and let out a silent groan. Though she tried not to, she couldn't think of anything besides Homer. The last week had been fairly bearable, knowing she would return to him on Tuesday. She'd even managed to stay off Clancy's radar for most of the week.

Normally she got poor grades on purpose. She'd learned years ago to do just enough so the other kids wouldn't tease her for being a "know-it-all" or have the teachers accuse her of cheating. Lately, she struggled for real, barely squeaking out Ds in science and history. She couldn't concentrate. Except in English. When Miss Elizabeth handed back her paper with a bright green "A" on top, she'd smiled, a cozy, warm feeling filling her. It was hard to write a bad poem when it was something she liked as much as she did Homer.

Finally it was time. Tuesday morning. Tara shook with excitement as she waited for the school van with the rest of the students. She was on her way to see Homer again. And, to make it even better, Clancy had been sick yesterday and there was still no sign of him today. She'd have Homer all to herself again!

She took her seat in the far back of the van, not caring they always seemed to push her to the back. Nothing could spoil her mood today. Outside, a loud voice called out and footsteps clomped down the sidewalk.

"Yo, dude," Jon called out the window. "We thought you were like half-dead."

Clancy grunted. "Nah. Just didn't want to take that history test yesterday." He shoved his way into the van and plopped down.

Tara's smile slid off her face. Nothing could spoil her day, except him. She huddled in the corner, staying as quiet as she could. The closer they got to the farm, the more her anticipation grew. Even the jeers and leers from Clancy couldn't drive it away. Once at the farm, she forced herself to stay behind the other kids, walking slowly, hiding behind her hair so they wouldn't see the smile on her face. After putting on her boots and grabbing a helmet, she headed to the horse's stalls where the volunteers had the horses already waiting.

She brushed Homer's gray hide, breathing in the musty smells of the barn as Clancy made retching noises behind her back. Though nothing could shake the delight she felt being near Homer again. Remembering Cindy's instructions, she bridled and saddled him, cinching the English saddle tight upon his back.

"Hey!" Clancy leaned against the barn wall, a look of surprise contorting his face. "You're done? How'd you learn to do that? You're usually such an idiot."

Tara shrugged. His putdown should have annoyed her, but it didn't. Instead, a sense of pride did a happy dance.

"Well, it's about time you're good for something." Clancy grunted and headed down the passage toward Philly and Jon, struggling to pull their horse's head down low enough to put the bridle on.

Tara chuckled and stroked Homer's face. He pointed his ears forward and stared at her. She half-smiled, staring back at her reflection in his dark eyes. This time she barely recognized herself. In her rush to ready Homer, she had pushed her hair behind her ears, revealing twinkling eyes. Her eyes never twinkled. She'd never been happy before.

"Hey, Tara!" Clancy bellowed from the barn door. "Robin says we're gonna ride today so get that hairy flea-bag out here. I'm going first!"

Tara shook her head and slid her helmet on, snapping the chinstrap. "Sorry, Homer," she whispered and, tugging on the reins, stepped out into the sunshine.

A horse's shriek rose from the smaller corral between the buildings. Tied to a post in the center of the pen, the wild red horse blared. White lather dripped down his neck to his legs. He reared, but the leather strap leading from the cinch-strap to his bridle stopped his momentum. He bucked and twisted, the metal stirrups slapping at his sides.

Tara shuddered at the sight. How could they continue to be so cruel? Couldn't they see what it was doing to him?

Cindy slipped up beside her. "He's Jeopardy's Double Trouble," she said quietly, nodding to the horse. Her tearful eyes matched the sadness in her voice. "Everyone calls him Trouble. Especially Richard."

Richard stood outside the corral, shaking his fists at the bucking horse.

"Richard hates him. And the feeling is pretty mutual as you can see." She sighed. "He was such a nice horse when Sam brought him last fall. Sam had him gentled and even green-broke without so much as a buck," Bitterness seeped into her words. "Then Mr. Jordan bought him for his daughter."

Tara took an anxious breath. She'd almost forgotten and

prayed it was only a coincidence this girl shared the last name as Alissa. Surely, it had to be someone else.

"Mr. Jordan said his daughter wanted to show Trouble in dressage."

Tara's brow knit in question. Dressage?

Cindy went on. "Dressage is a style of competition riding, a kind of ballet for horses. Trouble's sire, Jeopardy, was a Champion dressage horse. I guess Alissa expects Trouble to be one as well…instantly."

Tara gasped, her stomach constricting as though someone had punched her—hard. It *was* Alissa? Here? No, God, please. Not here.

Cindy's eyes darkened as she continued, taking no notice of Tara's shaking hands. "It takes years to make a great dressage horse. Trouble's a young horse. He's not ready for it. And ever since Alissa started riding him, he's gone mad."

Trouble stopped bucking and stood in the middle of the corral, his legs splayed wide, sides heaving. His nostrils flared with each raspy breath. His head sagged close to the ground, his tail dangling.

Tara's thoughts scrambled from Alissa. "So, why are they doing this to Trouble?" She jumped at the sound of her own voice. So not her to speak her thoughts.

"Apparently, they're going to force him to wear that fancy saddle 'til he's gives up and accepts it."

Tara narrowed her eyes. "You mean 'til they break his spirit?"

Cindy nodded. "Yeah. They've had it on him all morning. He hates it." She looked at Tara, her mouth taut. "Richard better watch out, though. When Sam gets back from town and finds out what's going on, fireworks are going to fly." She pointed to a tiny blue house barely visible behind the side of the barn. "Sam's the horse trainer here. Lives over there. He won't tolerate this kind of treatment. Trouble doesn't trust anyone anymore, not even Sam, because of what the Jordans are doing."

Richard opened the gate, a smug look crossing his face, obviously sure he'd won the battle. Before he could get inside, Trouble twisted and lashed out again with renewed vengeance.

Tara smiled, thinking to herself. *Good for you, Trouble. Don't let Alissa take your spirit.*

"Come on, Tara," Robin called from the arena gate. "We're ready to start."

"Yeah, hurry your skinny butt up, Tara!" Clancy shouted.

Miss Elizabeth and Robin both barked at Clancy, lecturing him on the use of language in class. As funny as it should have been, Tara couldn't take any joy in it. Nothing was funny knowing what Alissa was doing to Trouble.

"Go on," Cindy said. "I'll meet you in there. I need a moment."

Tara understood. It was hard to watch someone deliberately hurt Trouble. She knew how he felt. Turning to Homer, she scratched his ear and whispered, "Be strong, Homer. Be strong like Trouble. Don't take any crap from Clancy." A naughty thought erupted into words. "Maybe you should dump him on *his* butt."

Homer rubbed his head into Tara's sweatshirt. She patted his slick neck and led him to the arena where the others waited. She felt comforted being with Homer, but she still couldn't get her mind off Trouble.

"Okay, riders," Robin began. "Today, you will ride your horses around the arena. But first you must get on…by yourself." She pointed toward a large wooden box. "Position your horse next to the mounting block, so the box is on the horse's left-hand side."

Clancy yanked Homer's reins out of Tara's hand and towed the horse forward. Homer rolled his eyes and dragged against the reins. Clancy muttered and jerked harder, tugging him next to the box. Homer moved away. Again Clancy pulled on the reins, positioning the horse so the box was on his right side. Satisfied, Clancy stepped up on the wooden block and began to swing his leg over Homer's back. Homer stepped sideways, wrenching the reins from Clancy's grip and pranced away. Clancy tipped precariously on the edge of the box, teetering back and forth. Catching his balance, he shook a fist at Homer.

That's one for Homer. Tara pretended to fix her boot, hiding the big grin she knew covered her face.

"Clancy," Robin called. "I told you to mount on the horse's *left* side."

Cindy snagged Homer's reins and directed him to the correct side of the box, holding the stirrup for Clancy. He ignored the stirrup and jumped into the saddle with a *FWAP* of denim against leather. Homer grunted with the force and laid his ears back. Clancy grabbed the reins and perched smugly on top of the gray

Cindy stepped away. "Use your stirrups, Clancy. They'll help you keep your balance."

"I'm a skater. I've got perfect balance." Clancy put his arms out, imitating how he'd ride his skateboard. Lifting the reins, he dug his feet into Homer's round sides.

Homer shot forward into an unsteady trot, Clancy bounced up and down, arms and legs jerking.

"Stop," he yelled, trying to catch the flopping mane to steady himself. His hips bounced out of the saddle and he pitched sideways, rolling off the horse, tumbling to the ground in a pile of arms and legs.

Tara couldn't help it. She laughed. She slapped her hand over her mouth but it was too late. Clancy sat up and stared at her, his jaw jutting out, the veins at his temples pulsing. She swallowed and reached out to catch Homer's reins as the horse headed her way.

Clancy's hands balled into fists as he got to his feet.

Tara lowered her head, wishing her hair wasn't tucked so tightly under her helmet.

"Hey man, what a dive." Jon laughed. "You're better on the board."

"Clancy?" Robin called. "Are you all right?"

Clancy grunted and dusted off his over-sized jeans while continuing to snarl at Tara. "I'm okay," he muttered, shaking dirt off his black T-shirt.

"Good," Robin said and walked over to the wooden box. "Now that Clancy has shown us what *not* to do…" She paused. "You will mount your horses from the left side and *use* your stirrups. You do not *kick* your horse—you nudge with your heel."

Tara led Homer to Clancy and timidly handed the reins over, not daring to look into his face. Chewing on her thumb, she turned and slipped over to the fence, hoping to melt into the shadows of the tall ash tree. If Clancy could only get on and start riding, maybe he'd forget her. Jon and Brandy mounted their horses and walked them to the edge of the arena. Clancy moved toward the box, slower, a little hesitant. Or was he sore? Tara turned to stare out at the rolling pastures so Clancy couldn't see her moment of delight.

Once Clancy mounted Homer, he joined Jon and Brandy at the fence. The horses plodded around the corral, a slow-moving carousel, their riders bouncing, arms and legs flopping.

"Okay, trot your horses," Robin instructed. "Grip with your thighs."

The three students half-heartedly prodded their horses, joking back and forth. Even Clancy seemed to have brushed off his fall. No matter how hard they tried, no one was able to persuade their mounts to trot.

"Come on, guys," Robin snapped. "Can't you work with your horses?"

A nervous shudder joggled Tara. This was obviously harder than she thought. Would *she* be able to get Homer to trot? Was she getting her hopes up too high?

"Okay, time to switch riders," Robin yelled, an irritated edge to her voice.

Tara's nervousness transformed into anxious butterflies. .

"Here," Clancy snorted, flinging Homer's reins at her feet. "You thought it was so funny when I fell. Let's see you do half as good."

"Yeah," Jon agreed, slapping a hand on Clancy's back. "She'll fall off, for sure. And then she'll be even flatter."

"Good one," Clancy cackled.

Tara took a deep breath. Don't show emotion. Can't show emotion. Don't want to give Clancy any more reasons to clobber her. She stared at the ground and waited for the boys to move away.

Homer nuzzled her arm. His warm breath felt good. She tried to relax as she turned to the box. Her mind buzzed. So many things to remember. Left side, feet in stirrups, nudge, don't kick. Simone had already mounted her horse and Philly was struggling to pull his baggy pants up enough to swing his leg over his.

Tara wiped a sweaty hand on her worn jeans. They might not be fashionable, but at least they were practical for riding. She stepped up on the wooden box, her hands and legs trembling. Homer stood patiently as she collected the reins the way Cindy had shown her. She stepped into the silver stirrup and swung her right leg in a large arch over the gray back. Settling lightly into the scoop of the saddle, she placed her right foot in the free stirrup and let out a nervous breath. She was on. Homer turned and sniffed at the toe of her boot.

Tara nudged Homer with her heel and smiled when he stepped forward on cue.

"Good job, Tara," Cindy called.

Tara's cheeks warmed. "Thanks."

She reined Homer to circle the arena, feeling his strength, even in his walk. Solid. Powerful. His muscles rippled. His ears pricked forward. She swayed in rhythm to his body, peaceful, calm, confident, drinking in the fresh air and the smell of plowed earth. The trees surrounding the arena seemed to come alive. Sunlight glistened between the leaves like liquid sliver. Robins whistled to each other and hopped among the branches. Could heaven be any better than this? She thought not.

"Trot your horses," Robin called.

Tara nudged Homer with her heel as Robin had shown. Homer shifted into a slow trot. Remembering Robin's words, "grip with your thighs," she squeezed, balancing in the middle of the saddle.

"Very good, Tara," Robin called again. "Simone, Philly, can't you get your horses to cooperate?"

Tara trotted Homer past Cindy. Cindy smiled and nodded. A new warmth filled her. Not only did she feel a connection with Homer, she felt something with Cindy. Never before had an adult made her feel so special. Never before had *anyone* made her feel special. Except for Grandma Kay.

"Tara," Robin called again. "Since you've obviously ridden before…why don't you show the other kids a canter?"

Canter? Tara's mind raced. Cindy made a rolling motion with her hands.

Tara swallowed. Canter.

Homer's ears flickered.

Tara leaned forward as Cindy gestured and nudged Homer again with her heel. Her shoulders stiffened and she braced for what might come next. Would he buck? Would she fall off? Did it hurt to break an arm or leg?

Homer's shoulders rose as he pushed his front legs out in front of him, breaking into a lope around the corral. Tara's heart skipped. The smooth gait of the gray rolled under her. The ground blurred and long strands of black mane flowed over her hands as they breezed around the arena. Homer's shoulders pumped and the faint clop of his hooves hitting the ground resonated in Tara's ears. She didn't ever want this ever to end.

"Okay, you can stop and bring him in," Robin called.

With a heavy sigh, Tara pulled Homer to a walk, heading to where Cindy sat on the top rail, clapping, a wide smile on her face. Homer grunted and blew out a breath, shaking his head.

"You never told me you knew how to ride," Cindy said, her eyes shining.

Tara looked down, feeling a blush rise to her face. "I don't. I've never been on a horse before."

"You're kidding." Cindy rubbed Homer's nose. "You're a natural then. With a few riding lessons, you could be really good."

Lessons? Really good? Tara's heart skipped, watching Cindy move on to help Simone untangle her horse's reins. Tara couldn't help but wonder if it would be possible to come back and ride at the farm once the program was over? And take lessons? A glimmer of hope snuck into her thoughts.

But just as quick as the glimmer had risen, it disappeared, like a mouse into its mouse hole. Tara's shoulders slumped, reality slapping her over the head. Where would she ever get money for lessons? And how would she get out to the farm? June would never *waste* her time or money riding lessons.

"Get out of the way!" a man yelled from the other side of the arena fence.

The sound of galloping hooves and angry shouts scattered Tara's thoughts. Trouble hurtled down the lane, Richard and

Sam raced after him. Richard stopped in the middle of the road, chest heaving and glaring at the fleeing horse. Sam continued running after Trouble in a futile attempt to catch him.

The world seemed to stop. The only thing moving was Trouble, bursting through the open gate into the ring, the fancy saddle askew on his side, the stirrups slapping up and down, beating at his red hide. Clancy and Brandy scrambled up the board rails of the fence, barely getting out of reach as Trouble charged by, bucking and kicking. Cindy clambered to the other side of the fence.

"Tara," she yelled, terror shaking her voice. "Get out of the way!"

Trouble raced directly at Tara, a twisting, bucking ball of fury. Tara opened her mouth to scream. Nothing would come out.

CHAPTER SEVEN

Trouble hurtled closer, a raging red locomotive. Tara's stomach twisted, her lungs frozen. She couldn't move. She couldn't breathe. All she could do was gape at the angry horse tearing across the dirt.

"Get out of there!" Cindy yelled again. Her voice sounded far off, as if she was in a tunnel.

Homer pawed at the dirt, his movement breaking Tara's trance. His ears lay flat against his head, nose tucked so far back his chin nearly touched his chest. Tara tried to relax her hands, to relieve the tightness in the reins. Her fingers wouldn't uncurl. Homer thrust his nose forward and the reins wrenched free from her hands.

No! She grabbed at the falling reins, grasping only air.

Homer bolted forward. Tara pitched backward, rolling over the wide, gray rump, tumbling to the ground as Homer galloped away, spewing dirt clods at her and following the fence line, away from the frenzied Trouble.

Tara rolled over, blood pounding in her temples. She jerked

her head up, knowing she had to get out of there before Trouble could run over her.

Too late. His hooves thundered just feet away. Her life was over.

Trouble skidded to a stop in front of her. The reins of his fancy bridle cracked at her like bullwhips. He reared back, his long black legs slicing at the air in front of her.

"Whoa, Trouble!" Sam grabbed at the reins, pulling his front legs down to the ground.

With a quick jolt, Tara pushed herself backward, away from Trouble as he stomped and pawed at the dirt then heaved against the reins, pivoting in a semi-circle around Sam. His ears flat against his head, he snapped at the saddle dangling on his side, leaving deep, toothy gouges in the leather. Rage seethed from his eyes. Sam leaned in, and with a quick twist, uncinched the saddle, letting it topple to the dirt. Trouble lashed out, his large incisor's barely missing Sam's arm.

Sam shortened his hold on the reins, planting his feet to keep the horse from tearing loose, or trying to bite again.

Tara breathed in, her lungs finally moving once again. She stood up stiffly, slowly, eyeing the wild horse. Trouble snorted, nostrils flaring. She'd never seen anything so frightening. Nor as beautiful.

Richard stumbled to the entrance of the arena. "You got him, Sam?"

Trouble jerked his head at the sound of Richard's voice and let loose a shrill whinny, his body quivering with the force.

Sam's neck turned bright red. "Blast it, Richard, see what you've done? Why'd you let *her* get near him?"

Richard put his hands on his hips. "Well, she does *own* him," he bellowed. "Though, after today, I'd bet it's the glue factory for him. She never even got her foot in the stirrup before he near took her head off."

Tara followed Trouble's gaze. A thin girl walked out of the shadows and stepped up on the bottom plank of the fence next to Clancy and Jon. Tara's stomach wrenched so hard she thought she was going to throw up. It couldn't be.

It was. Alissa!

Looking as if she'd just stepped out of a magazine ad, Alissa removed the smart black helmet to reveal a neatly braided head of flaxen hair. Tan riding pants, crisp and creased, were completed by tall black riding boots, shined to a glossy finish. A two-foot whip dangled from her hands and Tara could hear the *FWAP, FWAP* of the square head of the leather whip as it slapped her boot.

A cold sweat popped out on Tara's forehead. She lowered her head, trying to pull some of her hair free of the helmet. A thousand emotions stabbed at her. Fear, anger, resentment. Why was Alissa here? Why now? She was going to ruin everything—again.

Trouble's ears flicked back and forth. His eyes rolled and he jerked his head up and down, tossing his black mane, frothy saliva splattering Sam's shoulder.

Tara recoiled, fear worrying her that Trouble would break free from Sam's grasp. Her eyes met his. Despite her fear of him, sadness overcame her. There was an understandable pain in his eyes. She knew it only too well. Trouble stopped his dancing, black eyes fixed on her. Could he see that pain in her as well?

"Whoa, boy," Sam said softly, his arms relaxing a little as the horse calmed down. "You okay?" he asked Tara, his voice hushed.

"Tara?" Cindy's whisper carried a note of concern.

"I'm fine," she whispered. "He didn't hurt me."

Robin and Miss Elizabeth watched intently from the open end of the arena as Cindy motioned all was okay. Robin waved back and turned toward the group of laughing students, shaking her finger and scolding, "It's not funny. We're lucky no one got injured."

A volunteer snagged Homer's reins as the gray walked along the rail.

"Sam?" Cindy asked, her voice barely over a whisper, "Are *you* okay?"

He was shaking, his face almost as red as the horse, eyes dark with fury.

"I'm stinking mad, that's how I am," he muttered. "They are driving this horse insane." Beads of sweat rolled down the side of his face as he pointed to Trouble. "Look at his mouth. The stupid bit is wearing giant sores on him."

Sam glared back at Alissa and Richard. "Dang that Richard." He rattled on, the words rushing out of him. "Alissa went to him 'cause she knew I wouldn't push Trouble how she wants. Richard'll do whatever she wanted, as long as she pays him. When's she going to see Trouble is *not* a dressage horse?"

"Sam," Cindy held up one hand, catching his eye.

Sam's shoulders slumped with resignation, his voice low and sad. "I wasn't here to stop them, Cindy. I wasn't here to protect him."

"Sam…" Cindy nodded toward Trouble. "Look at him. I haven't seen Trouble this calm in months."

Sam turned to the horse, one eyebrow rising. Trouble remained quiet, his eyes still locked on Tara.

Behind him, Alissa stood on the board fence, hugging Clancy's neck and running a finger down his cheek in a sweetly-sickening gesture. She motioned to Richard, clearly ignoring the incident in the middle of the arena, smiling like she was queen of the world. Tara's hands shook. She wanted so badly to rip her smile off her face, to make her pay for what she'd done to Trouble.

Sam's jaw tightened as he watched the group at the fence.

"Richard figured if he wore Trouble out, Alissa wouldn't have any problems getting on him. He'd thought wrong. She was already on the ground by the time I found out what was going on. She's lucky Trouble didn't kill her…or anyone else." He looked sadly at the red horse. "But Richard's right about one thing. I don't know what'll happen to him now."

"What do you mean?" Tara clamped her mouth shut as Sam and Cindy turned to look at her. Why had she spouted off? This was the second time she'd spoken her thoughts out loud. Hadn't she learned years ago it was better *not* to draw attention to herself? Yet, the question forced itself out. She had to know. "Richard wasn't serious, was he? Mr. Jordan won't send Trouble to the glue factory, will he?"

"Sorry, miss," The heavy sigh and slump of Sam's shoulders was enough to cause Tara to tremble. He gazed sadly at Trouble. "All I can say is it's not a good day for this horse. I better get him back to his stall now."

Tara fought the wetness that dared to spring at the back of her eyes. From the sound of Sam's voice, he'd given up.

Alissa laughed, one of her "I'm-the-center-of-attention" laughs, and whacked her whip against the fence. Trouble snapped his head in her direction and began his nervous dance again, bobbing his head up and down. Sam gripped the reins, holding him tight and turned him around, angling to the barn.

"They can't kill him," Tara cried to Sam's back. "Isn't there something we can do?"

Trouble pranced sideways and lunged, pulling Sam forward, almost knocking him to his knees. With strong, knowing hands, Sam clung to the reins, leading Trouble toward the gate. As they passed the rail fence, Trouble lashed out with a hind foot, sending Clancy and Jon scrambled back up the fence, fear etched on their faces. Tara wanted to laugh. But she knew it wasn't a laughing matter. It was merely one more outburst sealing

Trouble's fate.

"It's time to head back," Robin called and motioned to Tara. "You all need to take care of your mounts. Brush them, water them, clean, and put the gear away."

"I'll meet you in the barn," Cindy said to Tara. "I want to make sure Sam gets Trouble back okay. Tie Homer up like before and I'll be right in. Laura will help if you need anything. Okay?" She pointed to the volunteer holding Homer.

Tara nodded.

Cindy scrambled over the board fence and disappeared around the side of the barn. Tara shuffled toward Laura, taking holding of Homer's lead, glad to be back with her steady horse friend. Only her insides ached for Trouble.

Homer sniffed at her muddy hands.

"Yeah, see what you did?" A half-smile lightened her face as she pointed to the muddy stain on her behind.

Homer rubbed his ears on her shoulder and snorted.

"I know. It wasn't your fault." She leaned in and smoothed Homer's mane.

"Yes, I understand, Miss Jordan. I'll arrange it right now. He's good as gone." Richard nodded to Alissa and with a surly glare at Tara, headed to the barn.

The ache returned with a vengeance as Tara watched Richard hustle away. So, Alissa was really going to do it. She was getting rid of Trouble. It wasn't fair. It wasn't Trouble's fault...it was Alissa's.

Insides burning, Tara headed Homer inside. A small rock skimmed across the dry earth, smashing into the toe of her boot. Looking up, Alissa glared at Tara, a smug smirk puckering her lips.

Tara tucked her helmet in the crook of her arm, letting her hair fall over her face. Part of her wanted to claw that pretty face right off. The other part knew what would happen if she did.

Why couldn't Alissa leave her alone? Why couldn't she leave Trouble alone?

Clancy joined Alissa, slipping an arm over her shoulder. Tara couldn't get over how chummy they looked. How did Clancy know her? And what could she possibly see in him?

"Well, well, Tara," Clancy taunted. "Who's laughing now? At least I didn't *wet* my pants."

Tara tried to ignore them. She didn't need any more trouble. She couldn't get thrown out of the horse program. If she did, she'd never see Homer again. Her fingers tightened their grip on his reins.

Alissa tossed her long braid over her shoulder and stared at Tara. "I heard you'd be here today." Arrogance gleamed in her eyes.

Tara pinched at the rage within. Stay quiet...don't react...repeating it over and over to herself.

Alissa continued, her voice sickly sweet, in case anyone was listening. But to Tara, her words cut like knives. "Clancy told me you were in his class. So I asked Daddy if I could skip class to go riding, to see for myself. And, of course, he let me. He lets me do whatever I want. I think I'll come every week." She leaned toward Tara. "It's my duty to keep an eye on you and warn everyone just *who* they have in their class."

Tara choked on the fury rising in her throat. She had to get away. Get away before she said something. She took a deep breath and tried leading Homer around them.

"Yeah, you know it, Alissa." Clancy reached out and grabbing Homer's bridle. "Everyone needs to know so we can keep our eyes on our stuff with Miss Klepto here. She'll steal us all blind if we don't."

Tara glowered at the ground, her teeth clenched, afraid to look up, knowing both Clancy and Alissa would be able to read her face. Angry tears stung at her eyes.

Alissa laughed. An arrogant laugh. "Don't worry Clancy. I'll have Daddy fill everyone at the farm in." She turned and playfully tugged at his hair. "I'm sure she'll be out of here before long. Something's bound to come up missing and they'll know who to blame."

Tara couldn't take it anymore. "You know I didn't take your stupid purse," she hissed.

Alissa pretended to be shocked. Except Tara could see right through her. "Oh? Then why'd they find it in your locker?"

"You put it there. I know it was you."

"Tsk, tsk," Alissa shook her head, smiling her fake smile. "You know it wouldn't do well for you if Miss Elizabeth heard you talking to me like this, would it?" She turned to Clancy, a flirty grin spreading across her face. "When will Tara ever learn?"

Clancy grinned back, a sappy look plastered on his face. Tara wanted to puke.

"I need everyone in the barn…now!" Miss Elizabeth yelled from the barn entrance. "You still have a lot of work to do before you're finished."

Alissa brushed a piece of straw off Clancy's shoulder. "I'll see you later tonight." She eyed Tara one last time, spun around, and strutted off toward the parking lot. Tara noticed a dark stain on the backside of her tan riding pants. Well, at least Trouble got one good lick in on her.

Clancy swaggered toward the barn, knocking Tara's shoulder with a quick flip of his hand. "Better watch yourself," he murmured. "'Cause Alissa's not done with you yet." He laughed a wicked, evil laugh.

Tara leaned into Homer's warm neck, her whole body trembling. Why couldn't she ever get away from Alissa? Homer turned his head, enclosing her in a horse hug between his long nose and shoulders. Tara wrapped her arms around his neck, giving in and letting the hot tears stream down her face.

"Tara?" Cindy moved up beside her. "You okay? Everyone's wondering where you are."

Tara jumped and turned around. "No they aren't. No one cares about me!" she spouted. "You all just want to get rid of me."

Cindy stepped backward, her face filled with surprise.

Tara lowered her head, instantly wishing she could take the words back. She hadn't meant to take it out on Cindy. Cindy was the one person who *did* seem to care.

Swiping at her wet cheeks, Tara tugged at Homer's reins. With a voice as small as a mouse, she croaked, "I'll get Homer brushed."

CHAPTER EIGHT

Tara slumped on the overstuffed couch in the foyer outside her social worker's office. Glenda Ryder, her case manager, wasn't a horrible person or anything, but Tara knew she was just another number in Glenda's files of foster kids.

Fists clenched, shoulders tight, Tara closed her eyes and took a deep breath, her body trembling. The events of the last week flooded her mind: the appearance of Alissa at the farm, the near disaster with Trouble, and her own angry outburst. How could she have snapped at Cindy like that? Snapped at the one person who'd helped her so much? Cindy had hardly said a word the rest of the class time. And Tara couldn't blame her.

The week had gone from bad to worse. Tara couldn't concentrate in class and failed two tests. Jon teased her mercilessly. Clancy taunted her... "Alissa's not done with you." To top it off, her foster mother accused her of stealing money from her purse.

She hadn't taken it!

Tara let out her breath, grinding her teeth together. She

could deny it till she was blue in the face. No one ever believed her. Why would Glenda be any different? She kicked at the coffee table in front of her. Heaven forbid anyone think Amber might have taken the money. Just because she was June's daughter didn't mean she was innocent. Hadn't June noticed all the new clothes, the watches, the new shoes Amber had been wearing?

Tara glowered at the couch pillow. So what would it be now? She might as well let Glenda pack her off to another foster family. Who cares? She was so used to being passed around she never completely unpacked her two small cardboard boxes.

Tara tried to erase her foster mother's last words from her memory. She couldn't. They bit at her… "You're a thief and a liar. Nothing but trouble. Your mother never wanted you and no one else does either."

A hot tear slipped down Tara's face. She was not a thief. And she didn't lie either. Her thoughts turned to her mother. She'd been so angry the day she left. She'd always been angry. Hadn't she ever been happy?

Tara searched for a happy memory, a time when her mother might have smiled at her, sang to her, made her feel loved. No use. No matter how hard she tried, there were no happy memories, not one.

The office door and the foyer faded, a dismal back room taking its place.

Tara sat cross-legged on a worn rug in the middle of the floor. Large stains made gross designs in the carpet and the smell of stale beer and cigarette smoke permeated the fabric. Tara scratched out her homework as she waited for her mother to get off work. She yawned. It was late, but her mother often stayed after the bar closed.

The door burst open and her mother backed into the room, a shroud of smoke haloing her body. In one hand she held a small glass, half full of golden liquid. With the other hand she tugged on the collar of a man's shirt, dragging him in the room after her. She leaned in to him, hiccupping, and wrapped her arm around the pudgy man's neck. His face reddened as his eyes met Tara's and he pulled back.

"Wait," Tara's mother sputtered, reaching for the retreating man. Her eyes grew dark as she turned to Tara, her painted lips sneering. "You. What are you looking at? You ruin everything!" She kicked out, sending Tara's homework spilling across the floor.

Click. The bar room faded as the door to the social worker's office opened slightly. Muffled voices swelled behind it.

"I've had it, Glenda," June sputtered.

"June, please reconsider." Glenda's voice pleaded.

"She's no good…can't trust her…"

"Tara is not… Her mother…incapable of loving her."

June snorted. "I can see why…obvious."

The voices lowered and Tara couldn't make out any more as the women spoke back and forth.

The office door finally opened and June stepped out, an angry glare burning into Tara. Glenda followed, eyes darting back and forth from June to Tara and back. She cleared her throat.

"Tara," she began. "June has agreed to give you one more chance. She won't put up with anything else. No stealing, no lying, okay? No more."

The words buzzed in Tara's ears. She didn't know why she was surprised. She looked down and squeezed her eyes closed.

"I mean it, Tara," June snapped and turned abruptly toward the door. "One more incident and I'm done."

June marched down the hall, her heels clicking heavily with each step. Tara's shoulders slumped as she escaped behind her wall of hair.

Glenda cleared her throat and began to speak, her voice soft, yet deliberate. "Tara, I've received good reports regarding you and the equine program. You like the horses. If you want to stay in the program, you need to remain with June. I don't have another family in this school district to take you. If I have to move you, I'll have to pull you from the program."

A mixture of fear, disbelief, anger, and frustration clawed at Tara. She couldn't lose the horse program. She just couldn't. What would she do without Homer? Tara gave in to the resignation squeezing her heart, lowered her head, and shuffled after June.

* * * *

The next morning proved to be as dreary as Tara felt. Gray clouds filled the skies and the rumblings of thunder echoed. Rain fell in sheets, dampening Tara's hair as well as her spirits. Standing at the school door, she waited for Miss Elizabeth to pull the van around, listening to Simone and Brandy grouse about what they would they do at the farm with all this rain? Riding was out. The arena would be a lake.

"Hey Klepto." Jon bounded up with Clancy close behind. "Heard your sticky fingers are working again. June couldn't wait to tell my folks."

Clancy shook his head. "Geesh, how stupid can you get, stealing from the only fosters that'll have you." He grabbed Tara's hand. "You better keep these paws off my stuff if you know what's good for you."

Tara jerked her hand away and moved to the edge of the building. Rain trickled down the eave, onto her oversized sweatshirt, soaking her shoulders. She pulled her hoodie up over her hair and stared into the dismal sky.

The van honked and splashed water up over the curb as it pulled up. Tara groaned and shook her tattered tennis shoe, water squishing inside. She slogged to the van door, got in, and crawled into the back.

Huddled in the corner, she tugged at her hood to cover her face, ignoring the loud conversations between the other five students. Rain splattered against the windows, little rivers rushing down, only to be stripped from the vehicle by the force of the wind.

Despite the boys' ridicule, a shiver of anticipation charged up her back. She was going to see Homer. Even thoughts of Alissa couldn't sway her excitement. Visions of Homer's long gray nose and fuzzy ears paraded through her thoughts. She leaned back, wondering if Homer was as excited to see her.

At the farm, Tara jumped out of the van and ran for the barn, not bothering to pull the hoodie up when it fell. Homer didn't care if her hair was wet.

She rounded the barn door, glancing down the aisle, hoping to see the gray head sticking out of his stall.

"Hey," Clancy stomped into the barn and pointed a pudgy finger at her. "No five-finger discounts. Just 'cause you got the hair of a horse, doesn't mean you can..."

"Clancy!" Miss Elizabeth snapped, interrupting his sentence. "I think you need to work on watching your tongue." She closed her umbrella. "Tara, why don't you work with Simone today? Clancy, you be with Philly."

Clancy shrugged and turned, giving Philly a high five.

Tara couldn't help but smile as well, keeping her pleasure discreetly hidden behind her mantle of hair. Without Clancy scrutinizing her every move, maybe there was promise for the day after all.

"Miss Elizabeth," Simone whined. "You paired me up with Philly today."

"Well, I've changed my mind."

Tara knew she should have felt offended by Simone's reaction, but she wasn't. She actually felt sorry for Simone. They'd never been thrown together before. Why *would* Simone want to be partnered with her now?

Robin appeared around the corner, clipboard in hand, barking out instructions to the volunteers following her. Cindy frowned at Tara as she peeked over the head of a red-haired woman.

Tara bit her lip, leaning against the short stack of straw bales in the aisle. Was Cindy still mad about her blowing up last week? Oh, why had she snapped at her?

"Ready to go?" Robin turned and asked the students.

Tara searched for Cindy. She was gone. Mad or not, she had probably gone off to get Homer.

The thought of the grey tickled her misplaced excitement. Homer. She was going to see Homer.

Robin continued, "After you get your gear on, you need to get your horses out of their stalls, brush them up, and get them saddled. We'll ride in the indoor arena today...for obvious reasons."

An indoor arena? Tara hadn't expected that. It must be in a part of the barn she'd never seen. Anxiousness bubbled up like a shaken coke bottle. She was going to be with Homer. She jogged to the break room, easily getting there before the boys, and pulled the required hard-toed boots out of the bin and put them on. With hers on, she leaned over to help Simone as she struggled with hers. Simone eyed her with a whatever-made-you-do-that look.

Back in the corridor outside the break room, Cindy met Tara and handed her a halter and lead without a word, barely making eye contact, before turning and disappearing down an adjoining aisle.

Tara rubbed the smooth, worn leather of the halter between her fingers, the brass rings clinking. She wished she could take it all back. Cindy was nice. She hadn't deserved to be yelled at.

The realization hit her, a hard thump in the stomach. Cindy *was* nice. Cindy made her feel special, like Grandma Kay had...and Homer.

Homer whickered from his stall, his gray head sticking over

the gate. Tara smiled and pushed her hair out of her face, hurrying to him and hugging his neck. She may have ruined things with Cindy, but at least she still had Homer. She rubbed behind his ears, Homer grunted happily.

"He seems to like you," Simone said, gingerly reaching to touch Homer's nose. "The other horses never act this way."

"Homer and I are buddies." Tara hesitated, surprised with her loose tongue. Normally she wouldn't have said anything. She never let her guard down and talked out loud. Today she couldn't help it. This was different. They were talking about Homer.

Tara continued, a toothy smile breaking across her face. "Homer's great. You'll see."

Simone smiled back.

The next half hour flew by as Tara and Simone readied Homer. Tara shared brushing tips and Simone copied her. Soon both girls were flicking the dust and dirt off the horse, competing to see who could fling it the farthest. Together, they marveled at their success as Homer's coat glistened in the barn lights.

After they finished brushing Homer, Tara positioned the dark blue saddle blanket upon the gray's broad back and Simone lifted the saddle onto the blanket.

"Um, Simone…the saddle needs to go the other way."

"What?"

Tara pointed to the saddle. "Unless you want to ride looking at Homer's tail, we need to turn the saddle around."

Tara chewed on her thumbnail. There was a reason she never said much to the other kids, let alone gave them an instruction. It was safer to not say anything. To Tara's surprise, Simone laughed, thanking her for pointing it out.

A loud crack echoed down the adjoining aisle and a horse trumpeted. Tara recognized Trouble's shriek and peered around the corner to see Richard and Alissa walking the other way toward the outside door.

"He's tied good and tight, Miss," Richard said.

Tara could tell Alissa was angry by her walk. She rubbed at a red welt on her forearm and growled back at Richard. "Well, that'll teach him not to bite *me* again."

As soon as they were gone, Tara stole around the corner to the stall. Trouble stood in the center of the stall, ropes holding him securely in place, like a fly in a spider-web, barely able to move. The intricate bridle had been positioned over the halter, a mass of leather straps, rings, and buckles pinching his head. The saddle he loathed embraced his back like a swollen growth. His dark eyes glared and his red neck dripped with sweat. He stomped at the dirt floor, struggling and kicking the wall. Blood oozed from a bright red sore on the side of his mouth.

A silent sob stuck in Tara's throat.

"Isn't it awful?" Cindy spoke softly from behind Tara.

Tara jumped.

"I'm sorry I didn't say anything to you earlier, Tara. I've been so upset this morning." Tears welled in Cindy's eyes.

So that was it. She was upset about Trouble. Not mad at her.

"Alissa went to her father and complained how Sam wouldn't do what she wanted. Now Mr. Jordan has forbidden Sam from having anything to do with Trouble. They've put Richard in charge of his training." Cindy's voice lowered, anger spiking it. "Richard doesn't know the first thing about gentling a horse like Trouble."

Tara's heart ached as she watched Trouble struggle. Except, though she hated seeing him tied up this way, she was glad to see him—glad to know he hadn't been sold off to be killed—yet.

Trouble mouthed the bulky bit and kicked out, a loud *crack* following as he connected with the solid wood wall.

Cindy fumed. "Ohh, I wish I could..." She snapped her mouth shut and looked at Tara. "I need to talk to you..."

"Okay, everyone." Tara heard Robin's voice from the

adjoining corridor. "Follow me. The indoor arena is this way."

Cindy pushed Tara back around the corner to Homer and Simone. "Later. We'll talk later. You better go now."

Robin led the group down the hall and through a large open door to a huge room with a dirt floor. It was just like the arena outside, except walls enclosed this ring instead of a fence. Tara mounted Homer and walked him around in a circle. Even though her heart lifted to be with her new best friend Homer, her thoughts kept creeping back to Trouble. She had to do something. What could she do? If she tried anything, Alissa was sure to get her kicked out of the horse program.

Homer tugged at the reins, snapping Tara back to the task at hand.

"Simone's nervous to ride you." She patted his shoulder. "She doesn't know you're a big pussycat. She's going to love you. Not as much as I do, though." She urged him into a trot at Robin's instruction, relishing the connection she felt at his instant obedience. Cindy had called her a natural. But it was all Homer. He made it so easy.

All too soon it was time to switch partners.

"Hey Tara, got any more advice before I take off?" Simone asked as she slipped her feet in the stirrups.

Tara stroked Homer's neck and thought. She'd already shared most of her riding tips... keep your heels down, shoulders straight, hands steady. "Here's one," Tara grinned. "Smile and have a good time. Homer likes it when you're happy."

"Really? Thanks," Simone said, climbing aboard Homer. "I'm glad I got partnered with you today."

Tara stared after Simone, wondering if she'd heard her correctly. No one had ever been happy to be partnered with her.

As Simone joined Clancy and Brandy in the arena, Tara excused herself and headed to the restroom. She could feel the smile on her face and for once, she wasn't trying to hide it.

A loud *crack* sounded yet again from Trouble's stall. As if drawn by some force, she found herself at his door. His body trembled. One of the ropes had tangled with a hook on the wall, forcing his head high, holding it at an awkward angle.

Tara melted, sorrow and compassion mixing together. She clenched her fists as anger set in. She *had* to help him.

She glanced down the empty aisles, first one way, and then the other. No one. Satisfied, she unlatched the half stall door and stepped inside, latching it again after her.

Slowly, deliberately, she reached for the tangled lead. Trouble watched her, snorting, muscles rigid, ears rotating back and forth. Tara spoke softly as she grasped a rope, the cord harsh and scratchy in her hand, and untied the end.

"It's okay," she cooed. "I'm not going to hurt you, Trouble. I'm here to help."

She unhooked another rope.

"You're not trouble. No, not you," she continued in a calming voice. "It's all Alissa's fault. I know. I know how horrible she is."

She released the last two ropes and Trouble jerked his head back. Tara's eyes flashed wide. She stood rooted in the center of the stall, unable to move, inches away from the crazed horse—now a *free* crazed horse.

Trouble stared at Tara. He stomped at the stall floor and let out a shrill whinny.

What was she doing? He could kill her.

Splatters of red on the board wall caught her eye and her lips trembled. Blood! She peered at the growing wound on Trouble's mouth.

Compassion stabbed even deeper within her, overpowering her fear. He needed her help. She had to get that horrible bit out of his mouth.

She jumped as Trouble's whiskers touched her forearm. Her

hand twitched and connected with his outstretched velvety nose. Tara stiffened, ready to pull her hand back if she saw the slightest flash of teeth. He'd bitten Alissa. Well…she deserved it. Tara was sure.

Trouble nosed her fingers, his breath warm and soft, like a blanket straight out of the dryer. She stroked his soft muzzle, a nervous smile toying with her lips. As she gazed into Trouble's eyes, she felt the connection grip her heart. Without further hesitation, she reached up and unbuckled the bulky bridle, pulling it off, letting the heavy bit fall from his mouth. She reached to his side and uncinched the saddle, letting it slide into a heap on the straw floor.

"There. That's better." She stroked the blazed face, sliding her fingers down the brilliant white stripe. "You're not so mean now, are you? It's Alissa. She makes you crazy."

Trouble whickered softly, his muscles relaxing.

"How can you *not* be mad when she only wants to make your life miserable?" She stroked his red neck.

"Tara!"

Tara jumped and turned to see Cindy standing outside the closed gate.

"What are you doing in there?" Cindy lowered her voice, looking anxiously from Tara to Trouble and back.

A nervous shiver zipped up Tara's back. She was going to be in so much trouble for this. "I'm sorry. I know I shouldn't have. I couldn't stand seeing him tied up." She rubbed Trouble's cheek, her trembling fingers smoothing a ruffled patch of hair.

Sam sprinted up beside Cindy, gasping for breath. "I just heard…what Richard was doing." He stared into the stall, his eyes widening in disbelief.

Tara looked back, feeling the world start to spin.

"What are you doing in there?" Sam croaked, his voice barely over a whisper. "This horse'll kill you!" His eyes moved from Trouble to bridle and saddle lying in the straw. His face flushed, jaw twitching. "Not that Trouble doesn't have reason to kill someone."

Tara laid her hand on Trouble's face. "I had to get it off him. It was hurting him."

Cindy touched Sam's arm. "Look at her," she whispered, glancing back at Tara. "She's in there with Trouble...and Trouble is calm."

Sam moved in slow motion. He opened the gate and moved up next to Tara, slowly, carefully. Trouble pawed at the straw until Tara stroked the blaze on his face again.

Sam growled as he kicked the bridle out into the aisle. "I can't let you take the heat for this, young lady. You better get out of here before anyone sees you. I'll tell them I did it. I can't stand by and let them abuse this animal anymore. I don't care if I do get canned for it."

Tara stared at Sam, allowing him to push her out of the stall. Would he really let himself get fired for Trouble? Even though she'd taken the ropes off him?

She nodded and slipped out of the stall, looking nervously down the walkway for signs of Alissa or Richard. Trouble whickered to her, pawing at the straw. Sam grabbed at the ropes on the ground and Tara realized he was trying to get them out of there before Trouble got tangled. However, Trouble didn't understand. He reared up, ears back. Swiveling to the left, he lashed out with a hind foot, pitching the elaborate saddle into the wall with a loud smack before it bounced back next to the stall door. Sam bolted for the half-door, grabbing the saddle and tossing it into the aisle alongside the bridle.

"How in the world did you calm him down?" Cindy asked Tara, glancing back to Trouble. "I haven't seen him so quiet in ages."

Sam nodded in agreement. "He doesn't trust anyone

anymore. Not even me."

Tara's eyes misted. "He's not mean. He's just mad. I guess I know how he feels."

Voices filtered down the hall from the indoor arena, followed by the stomps and snorts of the horses. Class was over.

"Come on," Cindy said and hurried Tara around the corner. "We better get you back to your class before anyone sees you with Trouble."

Philly and Jon made their way down the corridor, leading their horses back to their stalls. Clancy's laugh rose behind them. Alissa strutted next to him, arm in arm, just ahead of Simone and Homer. She eyed Tara, a wicked smile crossing her face.

"So, you think you and my horse are buddies," Alissa sniffed.

Tara gasped, nearly choking on her fear. How did Alissa know? Had she seen her go into Trouble's stall? Was she going to get her kicked out for helping him?

Alissa pointed her whip at her. "Well, don't get too comfortable with that stupid old nag. Homer's out of here next week." She tossed her long ponytail and continued down the aisle, her sharp laugh ringing with Clancy's.

Tara bit her tongue to keep from shouting. Homer? She whirled to face Cindy. "What's she talking about?"

Cindy let out a pent-up breath. "I wanted to tell you. Homer belongs to Mr. Jordan and apparently Alissa has convinced her father to sell him. He goes to the sale barn on Monday. This was his last class."

Simone led Homer down the aisle, the gray lazily swishing his tail, totally unaware Tara was ready to spiral into a meltdown. A knot swelled in Tara's throat as the reality sunk in. She was losing her best friend.

CHAPTER NINE

Tara sat at her desk, her chin in her hands. Sunlight streamed through the large paned windows and bathed her in its afternoon glow. Miss Elizabeth stood at the front of the room discussing the population of the Proboscis monkey.

"Hey, they have a nose just like Tara," Jon quipped, tossing a wad of paper at her head. It bounced off and fell to the floor.

Clancy laughed and pitched a small bottle of glue at her. It landed on her desk and spun in a circle. "Urh, hrr, hrr," he imitated the sound of a horse. He snorted, blowing out of his mouth. "Thought you might want a souvenir of Homer." A wicked grin crossed his face as he pointed to the glue. "Alissa said that's probably all that's left of him by now."

Tara jolted upright in her chair and swatted the bottle off her desk, not daring to look at Clancy. Even if she wanted to respond, she couldn't. Her throat felt as if she'd swallowed a hot ball of molten lava. Large tears spilled onto her cheeks.

"Oh, leave her alone, you moron," Simone seethed. "Why do you always have to be such a jerk?"

Clancy snorted and stared at Simone. "Since when do you care about *her*?"

Tara glanced at Simone, almost as surprised as Clancy. She'd never had another student stick up for her before.

Simone shrugged. "She's not so bad. Maybe if you didn't pick on her all the time, you'd know that."

Miss Elizabeth tapped the chalkboard with her short pointer stick. "Clancy, Simone, can you please direct your attention up here?"

Tara stared out the window, her mind wandering, visions of Homer playing over and over in her head. Miss Elizabeth droned on... "Only the male Proboscis monkey has the large, bulbous nose..."

After class, Tara took her time putting her papers and books in her bag, letting the rest of the class file out of the room before she stood up. Simone looked up from the water fountain as she stepped out the door.

"Don't let them get to you, Tara," she said, wiping a drop of water off her chin. "They're jerks. They think they're funny, but they're not."

Tara swallowed and looked at the ground. How could Simone understand how she really felt?

"Well, see ya." Simone turned toward the outside door.

"Simone?" Tara chewed on her lip. "Why'd you stick up for me in there?"

Simone shrugged. "Like I told them, you're not so bad. You never talked to me before last week so I never bothered to talk to you. But, you're okay. And you're really good with horses."

"Thanks." A small smile crept across Tara's face.

"Well, they shouldn't have teased you about Homer. He's a neat horse. I hope someone nice bought him." She strolled down the corridor. "See you tomorrow. I can't wait to go back to Freedom Farms now. It was really fun last week."

Tara couldn't respond. Her eyes filled with tears and she leaned against the wall, hugging her book bag to her chest. Freedom Farms. It wouldn't be the same without Homer. Hot tears fell and she sobbed into her sleeves.

After school, Tara found herself confronted with a sink full of dirty dishes and four loads of smelly laundry. It was June's night out—"ladies night at the bar"—and she wouldn't be home until late. Though the chores had been Amber's responsibility, she'd saved them up, just for Tara, daring her to refuse to do them. Still reeling from June's accusations of stealing, Tara had no choice. As she folded the last towel, June swaggered in, making a beeline for the bathroom. The sound of drunken retching echoed through the door. Several long minutes passed and she charged back out, screaming for Tara to clean the bathroom, demanding it done—now! Almost midnight, Tara finished scouring the toilet. She fell into bed without taking off her dirty clothes.

Though Tara was exhausted, restful sleep was not to come. She twisted and turned, the bed sheets binding her legs. She could hear Trouble and Homer screaming. She could see them fight against the invisible demons as they were pulled closer and closer to their dreadful fate. They reared and kicked but it was no use, they were dragged, one by one, through the massive metal doors of death.

Tara woke with a start, bolting upright in her twin bed. Sweat soaked her brow. Her heart pounded. She lay back on her pillow, took a deep breath and stared out the window at the dark sky. A gray line crept across the horizon. The alarm clock ticked. Four a.m. Sighing, she rolled over and got up, tiptoeing to the decrepit table she used as a desk and pulled the lamp chain. Soft light filtered onto the distressed wood from the single bulb. Hearing a noise, she shot a look at her door, praying she hadn't roused anyone. June would be livid if she'd woken her up.

Tara's heart ached. What would it matter if June kicked her out now? Homer was gone. Did she really want to go back to the farm anyway? Her thoughts turned to Trouble. Yes. She had to go back there, for *him*. She had to find a way to save him.

She watched the door, and after several long, tense moments, breathed a sigh of relief. No one else was up. Taking out a worn notepad and pen, she scribbled furiously, journaling her thoughts until her hand cramped. Finally, she lay the pen down and watched the morning light force the darkness to retreat like a stretching giant pushing the blankets of night away. She yawned and moved to her pile of laundry in the corner to search for the cleanest pair of dirty jeans. At least Amber would have clean jeans today.

* * * *

The school van pulled into the Freedom Farm parking lot. Clancy and Jon piled out before Miss Elizabeth could turn the engine off. Simone chatted with Philly and Brandy, discussing last week's riding lesson. Tara watched in silent surprise. Not one of them had teased her on the way out. Simone glanced her way and smiled.

Outside the van, the air was filled with a fresh floral fragrance. Tara closed her eyes and took a deep breath. Not the usual farm smell.

"Enjoying the lilac bushes by the arena?" Cindy asked.

Tara tilted her head, gazing out through the mask of hair over one eye. She gazed at the plump shrubs across the lane. Pale, purple heads nodded in the spring breeze. She'd never seen a lilac bush in her part of the city.

"I'm sorry about Homer." Cindy gave her a sad smile. "I know you bonded with him. I'll miss him, too."

Tara swallowed, shoving her hands into her pockets, forcing her eyes to stay clear. "I had a dream he was killed."

"Oh, no," Cindy said, placing a hand on Tara's forearm.

"I'm sure he found a wonderful home. He was a good horse and well liked. Lots of people knew him."

Tara lowered her head to avoid Cindy's eye. No one could have adored him as much as she did.

"Hey, I have something to show you." Cindy motioned for Tara to follow her to the west barn. "You're going to love this."

Tara followed, uncertain. What could she want to show her? Especially in this part of the barn? Students weren't supposed to be in this part. She bit the edge of her lip and looked around to see if anyone was watching.

Cindy ambled through the large doors and stopped in front of an extra-large stall. Glancing back with a wink, she peeked over the half door. "Hey there, momma," she said softly to a tall black mare.

Tara moved next to Cindy and followed her gaze. Her eyes lit up. "Oh, he's so cute!"

Surrounded by a halo of golden straw, a newborn foal stretched out on his side. His short tail slapped against his bony hip, dark sides rising up and down as he slept peacefully. His large ears flicked dreamily. A fuzzy mane bordered his black neck and short white socks seemed to glow on his hind legs.

"He was born three nights ago." A smile brightened Cindy's face. "They named him Moonbeam."

The foal woke at Cindy's voice. The tall mare shuffled close and lowered her head. She whickered and sniffed at the foal's dark face. He struggled to his feet, wobbling on gangly legs, and stared at the visitors.

Tara smiled as the foal turned to the mare and suckled hungrily, his short tail flapping.

Cindy paused and tapped a finger against the side of her jeans. "Well, I thought you could use a smile before class. Guess you better get your gear on and get ready."

Tara nodded, trying to hide the pangs of mixed emotions

jostling in her stomach. She loved being at the farm. She felt at ease here—or at least as much as she could. And seeing the foal today did make her smile. Still, today felt wrong. How could she continue the classes without Homer? How could she ride another horse?

Cindy seemed to read her mind. "You know, you can learn a lot about yourself by working with horses. They each have their own personality and attitude. They react differently to different people and often act as a mirror to the people around them. Homer was a trickster. He didn't bond with just anyone. He thought you were special and I think he made you feel more confident. Am I right?"

"Yeah. I guess so." Tara pushed her hair behind her ear.

Cindy continued. "Horses can be intimidating. They're big and powerful and just like people, can be unpredictable. You overcame all that. It proves you are stronger than you thought."

Tara let the silence hang on the air around her, her thoughts spinning. She wasn't strong…was she?

The foal finished nursing and lay back down, his tiny sides heaving a sigh as he fell back asleep. "Guess Homer was a good teacher, huh?"

Cindy laughed. "Yes he was." She put a hand on Tara's shoulder. "Now, let's go see if we have another horse to teach you a thing or two."

* * * *

Tara and Simone followed Robin down the big aisle in the barn.

"Today you'll work with Rocky." Robin made a check on her clipboard. "Cindy will show you where to find him."

Cindy winked as she led Tara and Simone to the stall of a muddy-brown-colored horse. Rocky. Rocky wasn't like Homer. As the girls brushed and cleaned Rocky's coat, he swatted them with his tail. When they set his saddle and adjusted the girth to fit his extra round middle, he laid his ears back and grunted. They offered apple slices which Rocky readily accepted, but when they didn't have any more, he turned away, ignoring them, rubbing his head on his knee.

Tara tried not to let Rocky's grumpiness dissuade her. Instead, she enjoyed Cindy's compliments and encouragement, cheering on Simone as she rode, and trying to find at least one lesson Rocky could teach her.

With Rocky tethered in the middle of the aisle, Simone slid the saddle off. "Rocky isn't as much fun as Homer was," she said. "He almost seems unsociable, like he's ignoring us."

Tara agreed and thought back to what Cindy had said. "Guess he's kind of like me, isn't he?" She grinned and shrugged her shoulders.

Simone laughed out loud. "Yeah. Like you were *before* last week, anyway."

After putting Rocky in his stall, Tara cleaned the saddle and stowed it in the tack-room, breathing in the comfortable smells of leather, soap, and horse sweat. She missed Homer, and even though Rocky didn't have the greatest personality, she still enjoyed being at the farm and spending time with the horses. Cindy was so right, she had learned a lot about them. Homer had been intimidating at first—big and scary. He turned out to be as gentle as a lamb. And she'd found out she could ride him. Before today, she didn't think she could ride another horse. She had. Rocky wasn't as willing as Homer was, but she'd managed to get him to trot and even canter. She rocked!

She smiled, a warm hug of contentment wrapping around her.

Tara strolled down the dusty aisle, suddenly aware of how quiet the stables seemed. The others must be outside. This was a perfect opportunity to check on Trouble. She crept around the corner and headed toward his stall, stopping in front of his door.

The stall was empty. Totally empty. No straw, no water bucket, nothing! Except for Richard's pitchfork leaning in the corner. Tara leaned back and looked down the aisle. A thin line of soiled straw led out the barn door. Dread gripped her heart. Had Alissa kept her word and sold Trouble off, too? A chill shot down her spine as a horse's scream thundered through the barn door.

CHAPTER TEN

Tara stared at the barn entrance, her stomach twisting into a painful knot. The horse's scream from her dream echoed in her head. Except this time it wasn't a dream.

She dashed down the aisle and burst out the door, raising a hand to shield her eyes from the blinding glare of the sun. As she blinked, a shadowy figure in her view began to take form. Trouble!

The red horse yanked against the short lead tethering him to a white fencepost. A dark cloth covered his eyes, held fast by the gold rings of his halter. The pole shuddered with his jerking and the top board fell loose, hanging atop the lower board, sharp nail points glinting in the sun. Tara watched in horror. What were they doing to him now?

A gray rock smacked his rump and rocketed away into the pen nearby. Trouble reared. The rope pulled taut and wrenched his head back down, forcing his front feet to stomp at the ground.

Jon laughed as Clancy picked up a smooth stone and hurled

it at Trouble, smacking him squarely in the hindquarter. Trouble shrieked and lashed out with his hind legs, twisting and turning on the spot, ears tight against his head. He rolled his dark head from side to side, unable to see his tormentor and sidled next to the fence, screaming as the nail pierced his shoulder. It dug into his hide, ripping hair and flesh, blood spurting out and spotting the brown earth.

"Watch this," Clancy said and sprinted up toward the horse, punching him squarely in the opposite shoulder.

Trouble jolted, spinning sideways, his sudden movement shoving Clancy to the ground. Trouble's black hooves stomped and he lashed out with a hind leg, barely missing Clancy's head.

Clancy rolled clear. "Stupid horse!" He jumped up next to Jon and grabbed another rock from the ground.

Tara broke free from her frozen stupor. "What are you doing?" she screeched, as Clancy readied his arm to throw. Adrenaline rushed through her and she charged the boys, slamming her fists repeatedly into their arms and shoulders, knocking Clancy's stone to the ground.

"Hey!" Jon yelped, thrusting his arms over his head to ward off her pummeling blows.

Clancy grabbed Tara's arms and pinned them behind her back. "You stupid idiot," he sneered into her ear. "You are really going to get it now."

He wrenched her arms higher between her shoulder blades. Streaks of pain whizzed through her torso.

Trouble twisted and turned, his ears swiveling as he listened to Tara's cries, the blindfold slipping free on one side. Again, he lashed out, a black leg connecting with Clancy's pant leg. Clancy's grip on Tara's arm loosened as he gaped wide-eyed at Trouble, inching farther away to be sure to be out of reach of the enraged hooves.

Tara wrestled against Clancy and wrenched her right arm

free. She couldn't stop now. Gritting her teeth, she turned and pounded at Clancy's face with her free hand, beating him in the bridge of his nose with the base of her palm. Clancy squealed and released her other arm as well, grabbing at his nose as blood gushed out.

Trouble squealed and reared again, the rope stopping his upward movement. He pawed at the ground, blood dripping down his leg. Tara ran for him. Before she could reach him, a tall chestnut horse trotted around the corner of the barn and was yanked to a stop. Alissa jumped off and raced to Clancy's side, turning to glare at Tara.

Tara went icy cold, feeling like a bug under a microscope.

"Are you crazy?" Alissa shrieked as she fussed over Clancy's bloody face, leaning him forward and pinching his nose. She glared again at Tara. "You are in so much trouble this time. Just wait 'til I get done with you." She stomped off toward the barn, yelling back orders to Clancy. "You stay here until I find the teachers."

Tara squeezed her eyes shut, her arms going limp. Stupid, stupid, stupid!

Trouble twisted and turned. She had to calm him down. Easing toward him, she took his rope in her hands, talking softly, trying to mask the anger and fear in her voice, knowing she had really messed things up. Trouble stopped and listened, his ears flicking back and forth. She pulled on the rope, trying to slacken the line and untie the knot. Trouble refused to move toward her. He pulled back, digging his feet into the dirt. Tara reached forward and grabbed the cloth, jerking it away from his eyes. Trouble wrenched back, eyes wild.

"There she is Miss Elizabeth," Alissa said as she reappeared, pointing to Tara.

Miss Elizabeth and Cindy followed Alissa out of the barn.

"Tara? What's going on here?" Miss Elizabeth demanded, a

flush rising in her face.

Cindy gasped, her face going white, and hurried toward the fence to help Tara with Trouble. Jon stood and rubbed his shoulder, staring at the ground. Miss Elizabeth gaped at the sight of Clancy's bloodied nose and rushed to his side.

Clancy, head still tilted forward, looked out the corner of his eye at the teacher. "Hi wa' 'ara," he bawled and pointed a bloody finger toward Tara. "She jus' when' nus. She hattacked us, fo' no reason. Er an tha' horse are bot nuts."

Tara's mouth dropped open. She turned and stared at Clancy. For one of the first times in her life, her tongue wouldn't stop. "You were throwing rocks at him! Look, he's bleeding!"

"No whe weren'," Clancy blubbered. "Ah don' know how tha' horse hur himse' – we jus' come roun' and he kicked a' me."

"I saw you!" Tara yelled.

"I don't think so," Alissa snorted, a smug "I told you I'd get you" half-smile poised at Tara. She marched to Clancy and pushed Miss Elizabeth's hand away from his nose and pinched it again herself. "They couldn't have been throwing rocks. They were with me."

The incredulity of the situation hit Tara. Alissa was lying…again. A fire burned in her. She knew. Oh yes, she knew how malevolent Alissa could be. "They were hurting your horse, Alissa. They were throwing rocks and he cut him himself. Don't you care?"

Alissa looked defiantly back at Tara. "Are you calling me a liar? Ha! That's just wrong, considering who *you* are."

"Enough," Miss Elizabeth stomped her foot. Her strained face turned from Alissa to Tara. She pointed to the parking lot. "Tara, go sit in the van until we get Clancy cleaned up. We will sort this out back at school. I will not tolerate this kind of behavior. We do *not* hit! Do you hear me?"

Trouble stamped at the bloodied ground and pulled against

Cindy's attempts to untie the rope. Tara reached for his halter. "Please, Miss Elizabeth," Tara pleaded. "Please let me at least help calm Trouble down? He needs me."

Alissa scoffed, her voice low and threatening. "Trouble needs you? He needs your help like he needs a bullet in the head." She leaned in close to Clancy's face. "Seems she's as much trouble as that stupid horse is."

"Dey're bo'h 'rouble." Clancy grinned, and then grimaced as Alissa's fingers released their hold on his nose. "Tha' crazy horse halmos' kil' me. Near took ma head off an delibra'tly kick me 'n the leg."

Alissa's eyebrows shot up and she spun to face Trouble, an evil glimmer sparkling in her eyes. "That's the last straw." Her voice was loud. Almost excited. "Trouble is dangerous. I'm telling my father. He'll put him down. We can't have a vicious animal like this around."

Tara struggled to find her breath, but the air wouldn't come. Like someone had kicked her in the stomach. Tears flooded her eyes. Was this to be Trouble's death sentence? It wasn't his fault. Miss Elizabeth looked almost as stunned and speechless as Tara felt.

"Please, Miss Elizabeth," Tara said, choking back tears. "Let me help get Trouble to his stall and calmed down. I'll do whatever you want after that."

"I could sure use her help," Cindy croaked as she struggled with Trouble's taut lead. "She seems to be the only one who can calm him."

Miss Elizabeth's eyes followed Cindy's voice, her face finally breaking its frozen daze. "Okay, Tara. But as soon as you're done, you go straight to the van." She reached for Clancy's arm. Alissa snatched it away, leading him to the barn.

Alissa prattled to Clancy as they walked and nodded toward the chestnut horse. "I told Daddy I needed a *good* horse." She laughed. "I won't be caught dead on Trouble again. You can't show a crazy animal like him. So Daddy bought me Solomon. Now, *he's* a horse!"

Tara stroked Trouble's face. "Easy, Trouble," she said softly, tracing the blaze on his face. "It's okay, boy." Her heart ached and she choked back the tears. She was lying. It wasn't going to be okay. Not ever.

Trouble snorted, muscles relaxing as Tara pulled him to her, cradling his head in her arms. Cindy leaned in to untie the knotted lead, reaching to wipe her eyes with the back of her hand.

Tara blinked to keep her own eyes dry. She had to stay strong for Trouble. He relaxed slightly, blowing out a long breath.

Alissa finally relinquished Clancy to Miss Elizabeth and she ushered him into the barn, toward the restroom. Alissa sauntered back toward Tara, glaring at her, arms crossed in a haughty stance. "Poor Tara," she sneered in a mockingly sensitive tone. "Seems you can't win. You're never going to get close to Trouble, just like I wouldn't let you get close to Homer." Her eyes narrowed. "If I can't ride Trouble, no one's going to. I'll make sure of it. I'll insist Daddy have him destroyed. And he'll do it. He'll do it because I want him to."

Solomon wandered down the fence line, grazing on the grass growing around the posts. Alissa grabbed his reins and pulled him away, still glaring back at Tara. Cindy finally freed Trouble's rope and stood next to Tara. Alissa's face flushed slightly as their eyes connected, as if she'd forgotten Cindy was there at all.

"Oh, Cindy." Alissa spouted, the snooty expression returning to her face. "You can inform Sam he'll be hearing from my father. I warned him if he couldn't get Trouble to do what I wanted we'd get rid of him. And I know Mr. McDonald won't want a dangerous horse at his stables."

Trouble pulled against Tara's tightened grip. She turned and hugged his head, willing the sob in her throat to go away. It hung on, swelling like a soaked sour sponge. The sound of hooves clopped and faded around the side of the barn. Alissa was gone.

"Let's get him in his stall," Cindy's voice cracked and tears slipped down her face.

"Can she really do that?" The questions whirled in Tara's mind. "Can she really have him destroyed, just like that?"

Cindy shook her head. "I don't know. Right now, I need to get him inside and take care of this gash."

Tara pressed her cheek against Trouble's warm face one last time and led him into the barn.

After settling Trouble in his stall and helping Cindy bandage his shoulder, Tara trudged toward the staff lounge to change out of her boots. A heaviness weighed on her shoulders, like she'd been given a death sentence along with Trouble.

A white-haired man hustled past her and stopped next to Cindy outside Trouble's stall. His arms circled and pointed at Trouble, his voice low and gruff, his face red and angry as he pointed angrily at Trouble. Cindy's face went dark and she spouted back at him. "You've got to stop her. You can't let her get away with this."

"Well, he is her horse!" the man yelled. "Besides, he's trouble. He's been trouble since they bought him. We can't have him..."

Tara couldn't listen anymore. With a shake of her head, she let her hair fall over her face to cover the tears streaming down.

* * * *

Tara tapped the toe of her tennis shoe against the tile floor, the split in her shoe puckering open and closed. Perched on the edge of the straight chair in Miss Elizabeth's office, she waited for the return of her teacher. Her fingernails dug into the wooden sides of the seat as she mulled over the phone calls.

First, Miss Elizabeth had called Clancy's parents, then Jon's. Finally she'd called June.

Tara sighed. What would happen now? June would probably ground her big time and pile all Amber's chores on her as well as her own. Like she didn't do them already.

Through the frosted glass door, the piercing voice of her foster mother addressed Miss Elizabeth.

"This is ridiculous!" June sputtered. "This is the third time in two weeks I've been called away from work. I'll have you know my boss is getting really upset."

"I don't understand," Miss Elizabeth began. "This is the first time I've called you."

"Yes, well…" June paused. "Well, *my* daughter needed me last week…false accusations," she snapped.

Tara frowned. False accusations? Right.

"Well, what has Tara done now?" June's voice rose. "I tell you, I am not going to be called away from work because *she* can't keep out of trouble."

Tara closed her eyes and lowered her head. Had she really expected anything else from June?

A man's voice added to the mixture in hall. "What's the meaning of this?" he bellowed. "Where's Clancy?"

Tara jerked at the angry voices. The silhouettes of a rather large, round man and smaller, pudgy woman with flipped hair loomed in the etched windows.

"'ere I am, Da'," Clancy's called, his shadow joining the others.

The man yanked Clancy close so the shadows of their faces were one. "What's the meaning of calling me out of work? You let a stupid little girl whoop you? You little wuss."

Tara couldn't help it—a touch of sadness squirmed inside for Clancy. His dad was almost as bad as June.

More voices and hurried footsteps echoed in the hall. A

man's angry voice drifted down the hall. "Jon. What's this all about? They pulled me out of an important meeting. It better be good."

Tara held her breath. Seemed they were all here. And none of them were happy.

The ancient knob turned and the door squeaked open to reveal a group of enraged faces, all staring directly at her as Miss Elizabeth led them into the room.

Tara swallowed, sliding further down into the chair, wishing she could melt into the wood. The mob continued to glower at her, their faces dark, eyes narrowed, jaw lines rigid.

"What…have…you…done?" June shrieked at her. Her voice grew higher and louder with each syllable. "You're nothing but trouble. You hear me? Trouble!"

Miss Elizabeth raised her hands to quiet the group.

"Bu' she hi' me, Mish E," Clancy joined in. "She hi' me fo' no reashon. She bhroke ma nos'."

"Can we please calm down?" Miss Elizabeth interjected.

"I want her punished," Clancy's father chimed in, the fleshy bulge of neck pushing out of the top of his shirt turning bright red. "You can't allow this kind of thing to happen."

Tara jumped up and opened her mouth. She had to stand up for herself. Stand up for Trouble. "The boys were throwing…"

"You've got to do something," a thin woman added, smacking her hand against Miss Elizabeth's stained desk.

"They hit Trouble…"

"She's out of control," Clancy's mom shouted.

"I was trying…"

The uproar continued as the parents and Clancy all shouted at once, pointing to Tara. No matter how hard she tried to get the truth out, she was cut off with each start of a new sentence. Jon was the only silent one in the room.

Miss Elizabeth moved behind her desk and sat in her large

roller chair, trying to get everyone to follow her example.

"Well, I'm done with her," June raised her arm, shaking a fist. Her voice crested to a loud screech. "I told Glenda. I told her one more time and I was done. I will not be responsible for her anymore." She leaned over the desk to Miss Elizabeth. "Call Glenda to come and pick her up. I will *not* have her back in my house. Never again."

A hush came over the group as June stormed out of the office. Miss Elizabeth sat in her chair, mouth open. Clancy smirked and glanced at his father. Jon stared at the ground. Quiet overcame the room like a tidal wave, suffocating the argument.

Miss Elizabeth took a breath and cleared her throat. She got up and walked back around the desk talking in a hushed voice. "In the light of things…"

The deafening beat of Tara's heart drowned out the conversation. The room whirled. This was it? She had no home…again. She was sure to have no school either, not in the light of things. A pain stabbed at her heart.

"I'll talk with the boys tomorrow…" Miss Elizabeth's voice filtered in.

And with no home and no school, she was out of the horse program, too. What did it matter anyway? Homer was gone. And now, so was Trouble.

Fragments of the conversation trickled through her conscious. "The proper action will…"

Tara's head pounded.

"I'll take care of…"

A thick fog filled her brain. She dropped into the chair, pulled her feet up and wrapped her arms around her knees. It was just like Alissa said, she couldn't win. Hiding her face in her jeans, she gave in to the sting of desperate tears.

CHAPTER ELEVEN

Tara picked at the hole in the arm of the worn couch outside Glenda's office, pulling the stuffing out and poking it back in again. Seemed she'd done nothing but wait in and out of offices the last five days. Miss Elizabeth's, the City County Building, Bonner Home... Now, she waited for Glenda, her case manager at the Child Support Services office.

Tara's stomach hurt. Her head hurt. Her heart hurt.

She stared out the window at the fire escape and for a brief second she imagined escaping down it, running as far away as she could. A lump formed in her throat. Where would she go? There was no one to go to.

Her stomach grumbled a loud protest and she placed a hand over her middle. She couldn't eat, even if she wanted to. She had thrown up everything since the incident.

Five days...seemed like five years.

Tara closed her eyes. The events replayed in her mind. After June and the families had left the school, the rest of the day had drifted in a foggy haze. She'd wanted to tell her side of the story, but her tongue had given up. Instead, she sat mute, her past reminding her Miss Elizabeth wouldn't believe her anyway. Nobody ever believed her. And Trouble had already been given his death sentence. So it didn't matter what she said.

She sniffed.

Miss Elizabeth had called Child Services and Tara vaguely remembered walking to Glenda's car, like a dead-man, her legs heavy and lifeless. She'd thought she was all cried out until she saw the two grubby boxes crammed into the backseat of Glenda's car. Everything she owned in the world. Tears streaked her vision as she slid into the passenger seat of Glenda's burgundy Cutlass, the ride dissolving into a memory, like the ending of a really bad movie.

Tara pinched the ball of stuffing between her fingers. A momentary flash of resentment wrestled with her sadness, arguing with her mute tongue as she gazed out the window, watching the sunlight bounce off the brick wall next door.

So what was going to happen now? She had no home. She had no friends. No real friends, anyway, since Homer and Trouble were gone. Freedom Farms was just a painful memory. Was she going to be forced to stay at the Bonner Home for misfits? Had her life really spiraled so low?

Tara closed her eyes and sank deeper into the folds of the stuffed couch. The door opened and Glenda stood in the doorway, a thick manila file in her hand.

"Tara, you can come in now."

Tara shuffled into the room and slumped into the metal chair beside the cluttered desk. Something deep inside stirred. The words she so desperately wanted to say burned on her tongue—a part of the new Tara, the assertive Tara. The old Tara, however, refused to open her mouth, keeping it shut...as always.

Glenda moved back to her chair and sat down, pushing the phone to the side and shifting a stack of papers to clear a path to

Tara. "You've had a rough week, huh?" She opened the folder. "I'm sorry things didn't work out with the Hansons."

Tara shrugged and picked at the frayed hem of her jeans, trying to avert the swell of tears rising to the back of her eyes.

Glenda leaned a little closer. "You've been staying at the Bonner group home, right? Is that going okay?"

Tara looked out the office window, overlooking the alley. What did Glenda care? It was as convenient a place to dump her as any. Would Glenda care that everyone hated her at the Bonner Home, calling her names and pushing her around at every chance? Would she care the kids stole her blankets at night so all she had to sleep with was a ratty sheet and a pillow with no pillowcase?

Glenda cleared her throat. "Well, I have a new option for you. I've been on the phone all morning trying to get it all sorted out."

Tara looked up, a tiny sliver of hope stealing into her heart at the possibility of leaving Bonner. Anywhere would be better than Bonner. Even back with June and Amber.

"Miss Elizabeth called me yesterday. Jon confessed he and Clancy had been throwing rocks at the horse before you hit them."

Tara sat upright. Jon confessed? In a flash, her thoughts turned dark again, snapping at the back of her mind, wishing she'd hit them more. They'd deserved it...for hurting Trouble.

Despair gripped her shoulders and she slumped into the chair again. Hitting them hadn't changed anything. Trouble was gone by now. Dead.

Glenda continued, not seeming to notice Tara's reaction. "And, since Jon confessed, it has shed a different light on things. We still don't condone fighting. I think you could have found a different way to have stopped them."

Tara gazed at her hands...the hands that broke Clancy's

nose. How else was she supposed to have stopped them? Say "pretty please, don't hurt Trouble anymore"? Right.

"Anyway," Glenda began again. "Miss Elizabeth would like you to finish her program so you can get back into your regular classes this fall. But there are conditions."

Conditions?

"You will finish out the program, though you will not be going to class. We think it is best. There's only five weeks left. I have a woman who has offered to take you in and tutor you. Then Miss Elizabeth will give you your finals when you're ready."

Tara leaned back. Was Glenda kidding? Someone tutor her...one on one? Wouldn't happen. No one would spend that kind of time on her. It was just another empty promise.

"And," Glenda said. "Because of this arrangement, you'll be able to finish the program at Freedom Farms as well. But you will work an extra hour each week with Robin on how to control your anger."

Tara wanted to be happy. She *had* been happy at Freedom Farms. A tug-of-war gurgled in her stomach. How could she be happy at the farm now? A mix of emotions stampeded her heart.

Glenda walked to the front of the desk and sat on the edge, watching Tara. "This woman even has a job for you."

Tara frowned and leaned back again. A job? It figured. Someone else wanting her to do all their work.

Glenda smiled.

Tara fidgeted at Glenda's cheery expression.

"It's not glamorous job," Glenda chirped, picking up the folder. "You'll be mucking stalls and feeding and tending to a stable of horses." She gazed at Tara, waiting for a response.

"Horses?" Uncertainty thumped Tara's chest. "I'll be taking care of horses?"

Glenda patted the thick folder. "Yes. The woman who has

volunteered to help us is Cindy McDonald, from Freedom Farms. She called Miss Elizabeth and it is because of them I've been able to set this up. We don't normally have anyone in their early twenties want to foster. And it's not the norm with her being single. We're allowing this on a temporary basis. I've heard there's been great improvements in you since you began the horse program. Robin says you work well with the horses and Miss Elizabeth is impressed how you interacted with the student she assigned with you. We'd all like to see it continue."

Tara could see Glenda's mouth moving but she couldn't hear any more words coming out. Her own thoughts jabbered at her from all directions. Cindy had called Miss Elizabeth? They'd arranged this? She was going to live at Freedom Farms? She could continue the horse program?

The glimmer of hope broadened, then in a flash, shattered again. Gazing at the floor, she closed her eyes. She didn't want to go back to the farm. Clancy and Alissa would still be there...

She swallowed.

...and Homer and Trouble wouldn't.

Tara opened her mouth to speak and stopped, her thoughts too jumbled to form a comprehensible sentence.

"And here she is." Glenda motioned to the foyer.

Cindy waved through the open door.

* * * *

Tara sat in silence, staring out her window. Trees streaked past the car, the fences blurring into one long continuous white line. The car slowed and Cindy turned into Freedom Farms. Nervous shivers rippled through Tara. The horse barns seemed to glower at her, casting gloomy shadows, reminding Tara of the losses the Farm had experienced.

Cindy led the way inside the tiny house between the barns and a green pasture. She directed Tara down a short hallway to a small, tidy bedroom. Tara dropped her grubby box on the floor by the twin-size bed. Light filtered in through beige curtains, illuminating a white dresser and nightstand that complimented the bed's headboard. A dark brown, swirl-patterned bedspread covered the bed and a stuffed Palomino horse lay against the pillow sham. A photo of a girl jumping her big black horse over a wood and stone jump adorned one wall. Cindy placed the second box on the end of the bed and sat down beside it.

"I hope the room's okay," Cindy said, picking up the stuffed horse and played with its ears.

Tara gazed out the window at the barns, not really seeing them. What could she say? The room was nice, but being here at the farm was tearing her heart into pieces.

"You were really quiet on the trip home." Cindy's voice was hushed, gentle. "Aren't you happy with this arrangement?"

Tara looked out over the pastures behind Freedom Farms. Happy? How could she be happy? With Homer and Trouble sold off...to be killed? She swiped at her eyes with the back of her hand.

"Tara? You can talk to me, you know."

Tara turned, searching Cindy's face. She *wanted* to talk...really she did. But why would Cindy want to listen to her? And how could Cindy understand how she felt, when *she* wasn't sure herself? She was mad. She was sad. She might as well be destroyed...along with Trouble.

Cindy stepped forward and wrapped her arms around Tara. Tara stiffened. No one ever hugged her...not since Grandma Kay, unless Homer counted.

"I want you to be happy here," Cindy whispered.

Tara's shoulders drooped and her body melted into Cindy's. Tears streamed down her face as she sobbed. The past weeks flooded through her, pouring out, an endless wave of emotion.

Finally, she drew a deep breath and pulled out of Cindy's arms, amiss with her loss of control. She never let her true feeling show…to anyone. "I'm sorry, I didn't mean to…" She stopped, mouth open, taken aback by the wet streaks on Cindy's face.

Cindy rubbed at her eyes, sniffing. "No, I'm sorry. I'm sure it's been a really tough week for you. I just want to help."

She grabbed a box of tissues from the nightstand, offering one to Tara and pulling one for herself.

"Thanks," Tara croaked. "It's nice…what you've done for me. I just don't know if it's going to work."

"What do you mean?" Cindy's brow furrowed with question.

Tara plopped down on the edge of the bed, staring at the floor. "I mean, what am I going to do when I see Clancy…or Alissa?"

"We'll deal with them as we go," Cindy stated, matter of fact. "Maybe it won't be as bad as you think."

"Not for you," Tara moaned into her lap. "Alissa hates me and lives to make my life miserable. I know that's why she wanted to destroy Trouble." The memories of seeing Trouble that last day whorled in her head and she winced. She gazed back up at Cindy. "You didn't even say anything last week. Couldn't you see Alissa was lying about Trouble? He didn't try to hurt anyone. They were hurting him. And you let her get away with sending Trouble off to be killed. It's not his fault."

Cindy hung her head. "I wish there was something I *could* do. You see, Tara, my mom and dad own Freedom Farms." She pointed out the window to the large house up on the hill.

"You work at your parent's farm?"

Cindy shook her head. "No. I *work* at the clinic down the road. I'm a receptionist there. I help out around the farm—work with some of the younger horses and give a few lessons. And, I volunteer for the horse therapy class. It's a great program and I love the horses." She cleared her throat. "The reason I didn't say anything to Alissa is my mom and dad have been struggling lately. They can't afford to lose any more boarders right now and Mr. Jordan spends a *lot* of money to keep their horses here."

"So, just because they have money, they can do whatever they want?" Anger rose in her as she thought of Trouble. "That's wrong."

Cindy shifted. "Trouble wasn't the same after Mr. Jordan bought him. He'd turned…"

"He obviously had a reason." Tara grumbled, not letting Cindy finish. "Alissa is mean! She forced him to wear that saddle and bridle, even though it hurt him. And who knows what else she did to him when you weren't around."

"I've never seen her mistreat Trouble."

"That's just it. You've never *seen* her. Nobody ever saw what she did to me either." Tara's grief swelled and she took a deep breath. "Well, it doesn't matter anyway. It's not going to be the same without Homer and Trouble. I don't know if I can stay here without them."

Cindy sat on the bet next to Tara. "Homer's a good horse and I want you to know I found out he has a great new home. A family with two little kids bought him. He's happy. And Trouble…" She paused. "You bonded with Trouble. You were able to connect with him when no one else could even touch him."

Tara stood up. "Well, I didn't do anything special. I showed him I cared. Alissa doesn't care about anyone."

Cindy's brows furrowed and she struggled to keep her voice from wavering. "I cared about Trouble. And so did Sam."

"But you don't know Alissa like Trouble and I do. You didn't know what he was going through, being on the wrong side of her. I've been there. I understand."

Cindy moved the box on the floor to the bed. "Well, can you at least try this arrangement? I think it will be good for you to remain here and work with the horses. You seem so much happier when you're with them."

Tara crossed the room and leaned against the window frame. She *was* happier... when Homer and Trouble were here.

"I know you liked Homer. You made a great team," Cindy said, following her. "You did a great job on Rocky, too. Did you know that no other student has ever gotten him to canter before?" She chuckled. "He's a grumpy old horse, except he teaches a great lesson. Horses communicate with body language and show us words are meaningless if our attitude doesn't match. You must have communicated something to Rocky to get him to respond for you."

Tara stayed silent. Had she really connected with Rocky?

Cindy smiled, a look of pleading in her eyes. "Will you at least give it a try?"

Tara stared at the floor. "I don't know why you're doing this." She paused and glanced up at Cindy. "I'll try."

Cindy's smile faded as her gaze shifted past Tara to the window. With a loud gasp, she sprinted from bedroom, her footsteps echoing down the hall. Alone in the room, totally confused, Tara turned to see what had caused the sudden change. A white mare galloped across the pasture, running as fast as she could. She slowed slightly and turned her head to the side to glance back at the road.

Tara followed the mare's gaze. A blue pick-up and trailer waited on the lane between the pasture and the barn. Behind it, Richard struggled with a lead rope, pulling, trying to force something into the waiting horse trailer. He pulled out a long whip and slashed it through the air with a loud *crack*.

Tara leaned forward, clutching at her sweatshirt, unable to believe her eyes as the animal came into view. The red horse reared up, striking out with rage.

Trouble!

C.K. Volnek

CHAPTER TWELVE

The screen door slammed as Tara dashed out of the house and tore across the lawn. Trouble snorted, trying to turn his hindquarters to kick at Richard and the horse trailer. Cindy was already there, in front of the pick-up, waving her arms and pointing at the horse as she argued with a tall man.

Mr. Jordan. Tara remembered him from school.

"Mr. Jordan, if you only…" Cindy's voice was drowned out by Richard's gruff voice yelling from behind the trailer.

Sam sprinted into the scene, grabbing at the rope in Richard's hands. Trouble shied away as the men fought. The rope slipped free from their grip and Trouble jerked back, tossing his head, whinnying his new found freedom. With a wild buck, he raced down the lane.

Mr. Jordan looked up from his argument with Cindy and hollered. "Get that horse. Get him before he hurts someone!"

Tara angled across the yard, toward the white board fence separating her from Trouble. How was she to get over it in time to catch him?

Trouble bolted down the gravel lane, his black mane and tail streaming behind him. Tara felt sick with fear. She knew where the lane went...to the highway. Trouble didn't know the dark pavement of Highway 68 stretched ahead.

"Trouble!" she finally managed to call out.

On the highway a UPS truck sped over the top of the hill, its gears grumbling as it picked up speed. Trouble raced past her, hurtling on a collision course with the truck.

Tara screamed. "No, Trouble, *no!*"

Trouble raised his head at the sound of Tara's calling, ears swiveling, searching the ditch.

Tara slowed down and shook her head, her voice faltering. "Trouble, come back..."

His eyes settling on Tara, Trouble, skidded to a stop, pivoted, and dove down the grassy embankment of the ditch toward her.

Tara's breath caught in her throat. She dashed to the fence, every nerve in her body tense. He was coming to her. Trouble was really coming to her!

Trouble slid to a stop at the fence and pushed his head over the top board as far as he could, reaching toward Tara. She let out a long breath, forcing herself to remain quiet and calm as she eased her hand toward Trouble. She touched the outstretched nose, a pulse of excitement jolting through her. She collected the lead rope and placed a shaky hand on Trouble's neck, gazing into his face. The skin on his neck quivered and he looked back at the group of people standing in shock by the horse trailer, mouths open in shock.

"Tara. Be careful!" Cindy called as she moved slowly forward.

"It's okay, Trouble," Tara leaned in and whispered, pulling Trouble's head around to look at her, eye to eye. "No one's going to take you anywhere if I have anything to do with it."

She sniffed and wrapped her arms around Trouble's neck. Relief and fear swelled in her throat until she couldn't swallow.

How was she going to protect him? How could she take care of him when she couldn't even take care of herself?

The men moved slowly, stealthily down the lane, like lions stalking a zebra. First Sam, then Richard and Mr. Jordan.

Tara clambered over the fence, keeping a firm hold on Trouble's lead. "You can't put him down," she yelled at Mr. Jordan as she pushed on Trouble's shoulder, standing firmly in front of him.

Trouble tossed his head, snorting and pawing at the grass.

With a flick of the rope, Tara looped the loose end of his lead in the halter, creating a makeshift rein and flung it over Trouble's head. She wasn't sure what she was doing, except she had to do something.

Trouble danced to the side.

Mr. Jordan reached a hand out. "Young lady. You don't understand. That horse is dangerous! It's a miracle he hasn't killed someone. My daughter says he attacked a boy the other day, for no reason at all."

Tara huffed at his words. He couldn't see what a liar Alissa was.

Mr. Jordan motioned again to Tara, waving her to come to him, to bring him the horse. Like that was going to happen.

Tara stared back at him. Mr. Jordan didn't recognize her. He could get her kicked out of school on a trumped up lie, but he couldn't remember her.

"It's not Trouble's fault," Tara yelled. "He's a good horse. Alissa doesn't understand him. No one does." She put a hand on Trouble's neck. She understood...only too well.

Pulling Trouble next to the fence, Tara stepped up on the rail and jumped onto his red back. Her eyes rounded as she gazed over Trouble's ears, rigid and straight. She knew it was crazy, but she had to get him out of there.

Trouble shuddered and lurched forward, leaping out of the ditch and onto the road. Tara leaned precariously on his bare back, struggling to maintain her balance, squeezing her legs. Before she could settle back into the curve behind his withers, Trouble reared up. Tara tilted and jerked back on the lead. As if in slow motion, Trouble's head wrenched back. His body tipped and they tumbled backward into the grassy ditch. Tara felt the long black mane swipe her cheek as she jumped and rolled clear. Trouble crashed into the grassy ditch with a heavy thud, legs thrashing wildly. He turned over and thrust his front legs in front of him to stand up.

"Tara!" Cindy's scream exploded the quiet. "Are you okay?"

Tara heard the crunch of boots in the gravel as the men ran in her direction. Without hesitation, she grabbed Trouble's lead before he could flee. Jumping to his back, she landed on her stomach, swung her leg over and sat upright. Trouble ducked his head up and down, a shudder running through his entire body, eyes rolling as he struggled to look back at Tara.

"Stay back!" Tara shouted at the men, clinging to the makeshift reins with one hand and laying the other hand on Trouble's shoulder, doing her best to assure him it was okay. She was okay.

The three men stopped in the middle of the road, still as statues, their faces showing their fear. Any movement could set the horse off again.

"Young lady," Mr. Jordan said in a low voice. "You need to get down and let us take that animal before you get hurt."

"Stay away. I'm not going to let you take him!" She lowered her voice, cooing to Trouble as he continued bobbing his head. "It's okay boy. We'll get out of here. Ride away. We'll…"

Tears stung her eyes. Ride away? And go where? She lowered her head, her heart pounding in her chest.

"I'm sorry, Trouble," she sobbed. "I've ruined everything…for both of us."

Leaning forward, she wrapped her arms around the horse's neck, not caring if he bucked…if he ran…if he threw her to the ground and trampled her. She had failed him.

Mr. McDonald ran down the road from the big house. "Mr. Jordan! Mr. Jordan, is everything all right?" A plump woman followed him, clinging to a striped dishtowel.

Cindy ran back to stop them. "Mom, Dad, wait!"

Trouble grunted and pawed at the ground as Tara cried, her tears flowing down his neck. Finally, she sat back up, patting his satiny hide and sniffed.

Tara surveyed the scene. The men still stood, frozen in place, tossing questioning glances back and forth between them. Cindy took her mother's arm, talking to her parents, pointing to Tara. Her mother wrung the dishtowel in her hands, a worried look creasing her brow. Cindy's dad took a step back, his face turning hard and stern, hands on his hips.

"I knew it! I knew she was going to be trouble if you brought her here," Mr. McDonald yelled at Cindy.

Cindy's face reddened. "She is *not* trouble. She's the only one who's been able to get through to Trouble. Look at her!"

Tara cringed as Mr. McDonald glowered at her. What was to come of her and Trouble now? She could only imagine what he was saying as he argued with Cindy, his hands waving back and forth from Mr. Jordan to Tara. Cindy shook her head and turned abruptly, her back to her father.

Trouble turned his head to sniff at Tara's leg, his eyes revealing a new trust in Tara. His muscles relaxed and he snorted, blowing out a long breath. Tara urged him out of the ditch and stopped in the middle of the road, staring at Sam, pleading with her eyes. She turned to Mr. Jordan, her eyes filled with tears. "Please, please don't hurt him, Mr. Jordan. He really is a good horse."

"He's trouble," Richard grunted. "Nothing but trouble."

Sam put a hand on Mr. Jordan's arm. "If Trouble is as dangerous as Alissa says, then what do you have to say about this?" He pointed to Trouble, standing calmly and quietly under Tara's slight frame. She stroked his sweaty shoulder as he nuzzled her foot.

Mr. Jordan opened his mouth, and closed it again, a baffled expression crossing his face. He turned to Richard. "Have you ever seen this horse react this way before?"

Richard murmured and shook his head.

"Mr. Jordan," Sam began again in a quiet voice. "I want to buy Trouble from you. I know you and your daughter don't want to be bothered with him anymore. But I think he deserves another chance. And this proves it."

Mr. Jordan frowned. "Buy him? Are you crazy?"

Sam continued. "Trouble didn't respond to anyone…not until Tara arrived. Look at him. I think he's worth saving." He glanced at Tara. "That is, if you're willing to help me."

Tara's heart nearly leaped out of her chest, fully aware of what Sam was offering. She nodded, a smile sweeping across her face as she hugged Trouble's neck again, savoring the warm flesh and horsey scent.

Mr. Jordan scoffed. "Well, it'll be *your* head if he hurts someone." He turned around and, with Richard following, disappeared back into the barn.

"Did you hear, Trouble? We've done it!" Tara whispered, slipping off his back to kiss his soft muzzle, her hands trembling. "You're safe. No one will ever hurt you again. And we'll prove them all wrong. You're not trouble." Wrapping her arms around his neck, she hugged him tight. "Maybe there's hope for *both* of us at Freedom Farms."

CHAPTER THIRTEEN

Days passed in a blink, the routine of the farm growing on Tara. She accepted her chore list, caring for the horses and cleaning stalls, not minding the early hours. Cindy was strict with her school instructions and Tara sailed through her homework. Miss Elizabeth had even sent an encouraging "well done" note on her latest English report.

Tara followed Sam's orders and moved Trouble to a stall in the west barn. There, he'd be closer to her, and away from the major day-to-day commotion of the other boarders. Mainly, he'd be away from Alissa and her horses in the east barn. Tara was all too happy to respect those instructions. She found herself respecting Sam more and more each day, eager to glean the knowledge he so readily shared with her.

"Hey, Big Boy," Tara whispered to Trouble, his head hanging over his stall's half door, ears pricked forward in expectation. He whickered, long and low, stretching his nose to sniff at her pockets for a carrot or sugar cube. Tara giggled, pulling the orange carrot from her sweatshirt pocket. "I think you're getting spoiled."

"Can you believe it?" A girl's voice grumbled, her voice loud and haughty, from the other side of the barn window. "My dad sold that stupid horse to Sam!"

Tara stiffened. She didn't need to see the girl to know who it was. She'd recognize Alissa's voice anywhere. Trouble raised his head at the sound of her voice, his eyes wide and crazed until Tara placed a reassuring hand on his shoulder.

"Well," another girl's voice replied, "if Sam wants to waste his time on him, why do you care?" The crunch of riding boots on the concrete walkway between the barns grew closer, outside Trouble's stall.

Alissa continued to whine. "Why do I care? Because! That stupid horse bucked me off at least a half dozen times." She stomped in the gravel. "That horse bit me, he kicked at me, he never did what I wanted him to do. He should have been put down."

There was a short pause. Tara stood still, her hand on Trouble's neck, hoping to keep him from getting riled up over Alissa's voice. One part of her wanted to rush to the window, to scream at Alissa, tell her to leave her and Trouble alone. She wouldn't. It was more important to stay quiet and not draw attention to Trouble right now. Not if she could help it. She didn't want Alissa near Trouble ever again.

"Well, it's Sam's responsibility now," the other girl finally replied. "If the horse hurts someone now, he'll be to blame."

"It's crap." Alissa's voice rose. "'I heard Tara's living on the farm now and Sam's even letting her take care of Trouble. Like she knows anything about horses. She'd never been around one until she was kicked out of school and forced into the stupid horse therapy program."

Tara grinned to herself. Alissa was right about that. It's funny how things work sometimes. If it hadn't been for Alissa accusing her of stealing, she'd never have come to Freedom Farms. How ironic?

The footsteps softened as the girls entered the dirt aisle of the east barn. "Well, Tara's going to be sorry she ever came to Freedom Farms," Alissa growled. "If she thinks she can come here and make me look like a fool, she's wrong. She'll be sorry. I'll make sure of it."

The voices faded to a murmur as they continued further into the adjacent barn.

Tara inched over to the window, peeking out. The girls were gone. Her hands shook, though she wasn't sure if it was because she was afraid of Alissa or because of the anger welling up into her chest. Alissa's words echoed in her head... "She'll be sorry. I'll make sure of it."

So what was she to do? Tara leaned back, gazing at Trouble. She couldn't risk doing anything. Cindy's dad already thought she was trouble.

"What am I going to do, Trouble?"

"Well, good morning," Cindy chirped as she looked over the stall door, smiling at Trouble. "You got out of the house before I could catch you today."

"Oh, hi, Cindy. Sorry, I didn't hear you come up." Glancing at the window, she wondered if she'd heard any of Alissa's conversation. Probably not. Should she tell her? A heaviness settled in her stomach. What good would it do if she did? Alissa would deny it anyway, and everyone believed Alissa.

Cindy reached through the half door. Trouble bobbed his head, watching her. He was still a little leery of other people, though Tara was proud of how far he'd come in such a short time. He hadn't tried to bite anyone since Sam bought him back.

Cindy didn't press Trouble and he soon stopped, reaching his nose forward to sniff at her dangling hands.

"He's so much calmer now," Cindy said. "If I didn't know it

was the same horse, I wouldn't believe it. Sam's pretty impressed."

Tara beamed. "I haven't done anything...really. I told you, he just needed someone to care—someone who understood what he was going through."

"Someone like you?" Cindy eyed Tara and grinned. "You understood Trouble and wanted to help him. And now I hope you see there are others who are trying to understand and help you."

Tara looked up. Cindy was right. For the first time in a really long time, she was beginning to feel someone *did* care. Cindy seemed to be trying to understand. Before Tara could answer, Cindy continued.

"I was so afraid for you when you jumped on Trouble. Then, when he went over backwards, I was sure he was going to kill you. And for you to jump right back on? Well, it was the bravest thing you could have done."

Tara straightened a length of Trouble's mane. "It wasn't his fault. I shouldn't have jerked on his halter. I pulled him over." She scratched his cheek and he closed his eyes, relaxing against her hand. "I think he thought I was going to hit him. I'd never hurt him." She looked back up at Cindy. "Since he didn't buck, do you think Sam will let me ride him again?"

"That's why I stopped by," Cindy said. "Sam had to fly out to help a boarder retrieve six new horses. They called in kind of a panic. He'll be gone for three or four days. He said for you to continue gentling Trouble like you've been doing. Don't move too fast with him." She leaned back and dusted straw off her T-shirt. "He said you could take Trouble out on the lunge line if you want. When he gets back you can discuss riding."

Tara nodded, trying to hide her disappointment. "Well, your folks will be happy to have some more boarders I bet."

"Yeah. Things may be looking up for them real soon."

"I'm glad." Tara moved the bucket of brushes, her thoughts going back to how angry Mr. McDonald had been the day she saved Trouble. She hesitated, and looked up. "Cindy? Your dad seemed really angry at me. I hope I didn't cause any problems for you."

Cindy's face clouded. "I'm sorry you had to see that." She stared out the barn doors at the big house on the top of the hill. Mrs. McDonald made her way out of the house, strolling toward her rose garden a little way down the hill. "It wasn't really you he was mad at. It's me. My dad's always been mad at me. We don't get along too well. I love my mom, but I've hardly spoken to my dad since…" She cleared her throat, her normally soft features hard and angry.

"Since when? What happened?"

Cindy gazed back at Trouble, sadness welling in her eyes. "Well, I'm sure you'll hear the story if you stay on the farm long enough." She sighed. "My dad's dreams for me weren't the same dreams I had for myself. When I was seventeen, I wanted to show jumpers. I had a wonderful horse. A big black named Jupiter. I trained him myself and wanted to take him on the competition circuit. I even contacted a farm out east to help me. I went away for *one* week, on a school trip, and my dad sold Jupiter. Sold him out from under me. He told me I needed the money for college." A tear rolled down her face and she wiped it away.

Tara's heart ached for her. "Couldn't you have bought him back?"

Cindy shook her head. "I checked all the sale barns…they couldn't find any record of him ever being sold. I'm sure my dad sold him to this guy named Stonewall. He was going around to all the farms trying to buy up horses. He bought them to…to butcher them."

Tara gasped, grabbing onto Trouble's mane, knowing how

close she'd come to losing him.

"Some people think horses are mere stock animals, nothing more than a commodity. They truck them across the border where it's legal to slaughter them. Stonewall didn't ever come right out and tell anyone what he was buying the horses for, but I knew. If my dad sold Jupiter to Stonewall, he wouldn't have gotten a receipt. Stonewall doesn't want anyone to know where his horses come from." She turned to Tara. "You see, I know what it's like to be in trouble at school. I did a lot of stupid stuff—skipped classes and had my share of detentions.

"My dad always got on my case. He wanted me to be more like my younger brother, Jake. He's a brain. School was easy for him. I think my dad thought if he got rid of Jupiter, I'd spend more time focusing on school."

Cindy leaned against the stall door, staring into space. "I couldn't be like Jake. We're so different. School was hard for me. I got tired of it and quit trying. I know it was stupid, but it didn't give my dad the right to sell my horse, especially to Stonewall. I hardly talked to my dad after that. I wasn't going to college. I graduated from high school, took the money he said he got from Jupiter and left."

"How come you came back here?"

Cindy's mouth formed a straight, tight line. She pointed to Mrs. McDonald, snipping and pruning the roses. "I came back for my mom. I adore her. She was diagnosed with breast cancer almost two years ago. Tons of medical bills. That's why they're in financial trouble. She's in remission now and since things are starting to look up for the farm, I'll probably be moving on again before long."

Tara bit at her lip. So this was why her stay here was only temporary. Cindy knew she'd be leaving.

Tara's shoulders drooped. She'd be dumped again. She wanted to be mad at Cindy, except she couldn't be. Maybe it was because she knew before she ever came, it was only temporary. Maybe it was because Cindy actually cared. Or maybe it was because she could feel Cindy's pain.

"Why didn't you ever ask your mom what happened to Jupiter?" Tara asked, thinking out loud.

"I tried a couple of times," Cindy sighed. "Every time I brought Jupiter up, she broke down crying. She seemed almost as upset as I was. So I quit asking her. It was too painful."

She took a deep breath as though she'd finished a long run.

"I'm sorry, Tara. Sorry I burdened you with my past."

"It's okay, I know how you feel."

Cindy tried to smile. "Yes, I'm sure you do. Life isn't easy, is it? But we have to learn how to cope and go on." She stretched out her hand again for Trouble to smell. "You've been dealt a bad hand, Tara. I could tell things were really hard for you. You've changed a lot since I first met you. The horses have been good for you."

Tara rubbed Trouble's neck. "I couldn't have done it without Homer and Trouble."

Cindy chuckled. "I agree. They're good teachers."

"So are you," Tara said. "You've helped me a lot through the program."

"Well I hope I can teach you not to make the same mistakes I made."

"Like what?"

Cindy sighed. "I'd always dreamed of training horses. I was so mad at my dad after graduation, I didn't care about anything. I gave up. Took the money from Jupiter and blew it and I've been doing odd jobs ever since." She stared at Tara. "Don't do what I did. Hold onto your dreams and keep after them. Don't let them die like I did."

Tara pondered Cindy's advice. No one had ever talked to Tara about dreams. Have-nots weren't supposed to have dreams, were they?

"Why didn't you ever contact the farm again?" Tara asked. "The one out East, the one you were going to train at? Couldn't you have still worked there? Trained jumpers or something? Can't you call them now?"

Cindy paused, dumbstruck. "Me? Now? Call Scarborough Farms? Oh, I couldn't."

"Why not?"

Cindy frowned at Tara. "It's been so long. I'm sure they don't even remember who I am, let alone have a spot open anymore."

It was Tara's turn to frown at Cindy. Before she could stop herself, she continued, "You just told me not to let my dreams die. How do you expect me to listen to you if you won't listen to yourself?"

Cindy's face clouded and Tara clamped her mouth shut. Where was the old Tara when she needed to be quiet?

Without a word, Cindy's features softened, a tear tracing its way down her cheek. Finally, she spoke. "You know, you're right. I've been holding onto my anger with my dad for so long it stopped me from moving forward. I gave up on my dream of jumping because I thought it would hurt him, but it only hurt me. Maybe Scarborough Farms won't remember me, but I'll never know if I don't call. I still have their number and they did tell me to call any time." She stared at Tara, her mouth tugging up on one side.

Tara smiled back at Cindy. She'd never played counselor before. She'd always been the one people tried to counsel.

Cindy glanced at her watch. "Oh my, Miss Elizabeth and the class will be here in an hour. I'd better get to our volunteer meeting. Bet you'll be glad to see Simone again."

Class? Tara's breath stalled in her chest. She'd forgotten horse therapy was today. There'd been no class last week and what with getting used to the farm's routine and taking care of Trouble, she'd lost track of the days. Staring at Trouble's healing shoulder, the memories of the last class flooded back—Clancy and Jon throwing rocks, Clancy's broken nose, June kicking her out...

Her stomach tightened. Would this class turn out to be as bad as the last one?

CHAPTER FOURTEEN

Tara leaned against the tack room door, watching a butterfly dance in the sunlight of the barn entrance. She enjoyed the quiet here, letting the shadows of the barn wrap around her like a worn blanket, wishing she could stay there and not go to Robin's class. She tugged at her ponytail, tempted to take the band out of her hair and hide behind her brown veil. She didn't.

"Hello, Tara," Mrs. McDonald said as she walked down the barn corridor, a small bucket of apples in her hands.

Tara jumped. "Oh, hi."

"I know we haven't been formally introduced. I'm Cindy's mom."

Tara nodded. "I've seen you around. It's nice to meet you, Mrs. McDonald."

Mrs. McDonald smiled. She had a nice face, like Cindy. "I hope you are enjoying the farm. I hear the horses are really fond of you." She leaned in a little closer. "You know, I trust a horse's judgment of character a lot more than I do most people's." She winked.

"Thanks," Tara grinned back. She liked Cindy's mom.

Mrs. McDonald shook her small bucket, the apples rattling in the bottom. "I don't ride anymore, though I still have my crabby old horse. He's not good for much, but he means a lot to me. I come down and give him a special treat every now and then. I think you might know him. Rocky?"

Tara mouth dropped open. Rocky was Mrs. McDonald's horse? She looked to the apples and smiled. "I know him well, Mrs. McDonald. I've been riding him in class."

Mrs. McDonald chuckled. "Then you know how grumpy he can be."

Tara laughed. "He's a nice horse."

"Yes. I love him. The crabby old fart." Mrs. McDonald puffed and wiped her forehead. "Well, I better go now." She waved and continued down the aisle.

Jon and Philly jogged into the barn, bantering back and forth. Simone and Brandy followed, casually making their way toward the break room.

Simone glanced down the aisle at her. "Tara!" A broad smile crossed her face and she raced down the passageway and hugged her. "You *are* here! Clancy said you'd be here but I didn't believe him."

Tara stiffened, surprised by Simone's happy outburst, then relaxed and enjoyed the hug, relishing the friendship. "I live here now. Didn't Miss Elizabeth tell you?"

Brandy joined them, shaking her head as she came in on the conversation. "Miss Elizabeth's hardly said a word. At first Clancy bragged how *he* got you kicked out of school." She pointed back at Jon who stood in the middle of the barn door staring at Tara, regret written in his red face and downcast eyes. "That is, until Jon told us what the Hansons did. Jon feels real bad for getting you in trouble like that."

Tara gave Jon a small smile, and turned back to Brandy and

Simone. "Well, I'm staying with Cindy McDonald for now. She got me a job here and is tutoring me so I can finish the semester."

"Great!" Simone said, smiling warmly.

Brandy grimaced. "You're working at the farm? Cleaning up horse poop and stuff?"

Tara laughed. "Yeah. Mucking stalls is definitely not like shopping at Macy's." She felt a warmth tug at her cheeks and tapped the toe of her boot in the dry dirt. "But it's great to be around the horses."

Simone grinned. "And I know you love that. I'm just sorry Homer and Trouble aren't here anymore. I know you really cared about them. That was so mean of Alissa to convince her dad to have Trouble killed."

Tara felt her heart stop cold. Should she tell them? Could she trust them? Alissa was sure to find out where he was soon enough anyway. "Trouble's not dead," she whispered, peering around to see if anyone else was listening.

"What?" Simone asked, her mouth hanging open. "Alissa's dad...?"

"He *was* going to put Trouble down. But Sam owns him now. Trouble's here. I'm taking care of him."

Tara laughed as the girls squealed with delight.

Clancy ambled through the barn door, kicking an empty pop can. He tugged at his sagging jeans, stopping short as he spied Tara.

Tara gaped back, praying he hadn't overheard and run to tell Alissa.

"Well? What are you looking at moron?" he seethed. "This ain't nothing. You missed seeing your handiwork at its finest." Clancy pointed to his face, light green streaks circling his eyes. From the looks, Tara could tell he'd had two black shiners.

Clancy lowered his head and shuffled on, glancing back at

Tara before entering the break room. This was not the reaction she'd expected from him, not at all. She'd expected him ready to kill her for what she'd done.

Miss Elizabeth strolled into the barn and smiled brightly. "Hi, Tara. I'm so glad to see you. How do you like being at the farm?"

Tara smiled. "Hi. Miss Elizabeth. I really like it here."

"Well, from the homework you've been producing, I think this has worked out great." She moved on toward the group of volunteers standing at the end of the aisle getting their instructions from Robin. She called back over her shoulder, "You girls better get your gear on. Class is starting soon."

The lesson flew by. Tara and Simone brushed and saddled Rocky, Tara taking extra care to brush his brown hide to a chocolaty gleam. She smiled.

Outside, the sun warmed Tara's back as they took turns riding around the arena. A pair of turtledoves fluttered from the fence to the roof of the barn, cooing to each other in their distinctive voices. A squirrel darted up the rough bark of a lofty oak, chattering his annoyance at the horses. Tara couldn't help but smile. Even Rocky couldn't maintain his grumpy attitude on this fine spring day. He quickened his step, prancing forward and tossing his head, as Simone gave a startled squeal and grabbed at his coarse mane.

"Horses are like people," Robin said from the edge of the arena where the students and horses waited for their next instructions. "They are social beings. In many ways, however, horses violate the basic principles of the street...where power is used to control. Horses are obviously more powerful than humans. They could choose to do whatever they please. Instead, most times, they choose to work with us and our strange requests. Will your horse cooperate with you?" She pointed to Philly. "Please ride your horse over the water feature."

Robin pointed to a two-foot wide stream of water the volunteers had created. The water sparkled as it gushed out of the hose and flowed down the shallow riverbed they had dug.

Philly stared at the water. "You want me to ride Geronimo over that? Why?"

Robin put her hands on her hips. "Just guide him through it."

"Ah, this'll be easy."

Philly nudged the black horse toward the small man-made rivulet. Geronimo stopped and snorted, dropping his head to sniff at the ground. Philly kicked his round belly. Still the horse balked.

"Oh, come on," Philly rumbled. "What's a little water?"

He kicked again, raising the reins to force the horse over the small stretch of mud and water. Geronimo side-stepped, gave a little hop and trotted the opposite way, a red-faced Philly grabbing onto the front of the saddle to save his seat.

Robin grinned. "Simone, would you try? As you can see, horses are cautious creatures. They may wonder how deep the water is, or if it's a trap. Can you get your horse to trust you?"

Simone looked to Tara, eyes wide.

"You can do it," Tara whispered. "Just work with Rocky. Be patient. Let him sort it out before pushing him to go over it. Don't try to force him like Philly did."

Simone turned Rocky toward the water. She walked him to the edge and let him drop his large head to sniff at the imitation stream. Nudging him with her heel and holding the reins steady, she clucked to him, coaxing him forward. Rocky snorted and stepped into the mud, shaking his head in a bored manner.

A round of applause broke out from Robin and the volunteers.

"Good job," Cindy cheered from her spot on the fence.

Simone beamed at Tara.

One by one, the students took their turns. Brandy was next to try and get Cinnamon through it. She nearly fell off when the red roan horse decided to jump the rivulet rather than walk through it. Rocky seemed more interested in the water when Tara took her turn. He pawed at the water, splashing and stamping, before she could coax him all the way through it. Silly old horse, Tara thought. Jon went after her and rode Cinnamon through with no problems.

Clancy was last. He straddled Geronimo rather precariously as his sagging jeans wouldn't allow him to sit straight in the saddle. He edged the black horse to the water, allowing him to sniff at it like he'd watched the others do. With a smug smile embellishing his face, he nodded at Simone and Brandy.

Geronimo stepped into the middle of the stream and stopped.

Clancy stared down at the black's head, his smile turning into a scowl. He kicked. The horse wouldn't budge. Instead Geronimo buckled his front legs and knelt down into the mud. Clancy fell forward and grabbed the horse's neck so as not to fall off. Geronimo lowered his back legs until he lay in the middle of the water feature.

"Get off him," Clancy's volunteer yelled. "Get off! He's going to roll!"

With a loud grunt of pleasure, Geronimo pushed his legs out and began to turn over. Clancy bounced out of the saddle, landing in the middle of the mud with a big splash.

As Clancy stood up, his oversized jeans slipped down to his knees, displaying a pair of green-striped boxers. The students burst into a round of laughter. Clancy grabbed at his jeans, slipping and sliding in the mud, a red blush rushing up through his face. He tugged the denims up and stormed off to the barn, leaving Philly and the volunteer to pull the muddy Geronimo out of the fake stream.

After class, the students headed to the break room to return their boots and helmets to the proper tubs. Everyone except Tara. Boots were her normal shoe these days. She led Rocky outside to get a drink of water before she turned him back out to pasture. The sun shimmered on the water in the horse trough. Jon and Philly sauntered toward the parking lot, Jon waving and dancing a silly step. Brandy jogged to catch up with the boys, turned, and yelled goodbye. Tara grinned and waved back.

Simone joined Tara at the trough and patted Rocky's brown neck. She pushed her dark hair behind her ear and looked up at Tara. "I'm really glad you're back...here at least. You've turned out to be a pretty cool friend." She waved good-bye and headed toward the van. "See you next week."

A lump rose in Tara's throat. Only this time, the lump wasn't fear, or anger. It was joy. Pure joy. Simone had called her friend. A wide smile spread across her face.

Clancy walked past, his shoulders hunched forward. Mud still clung to his pant legs and his T-shirt sported a new design.

"Are you okay, Clancy?" Tara asked. She quickly closed her mouth, unsure why she couldn't control her tongue, wondering if Clancy would turn this around to be her fault again.

Clancy stared back at her, eyes narrowed, brows twisted together.

Tara swallowed. "That could have happened to any of us. Like people, horses can be a little unpredictable, huh?"

A crimson blush crept up Clancy's face. He opened his mouth then shut it as the voice of Miss Elizabeth filtered out of the barn.

"See you next week, Robin."

Clancy wheeled around and marched off to the van.

Tara's stomach did a quick flip-flop. Why had she said anything? Especially something nice?

She couldn't help but feel sorry for Clancy. What with all the kids laughing, she'd have wanted to crawl under a rock herself.

Rocky turned his head, slobbering water onto Tara's arm. She jumped and playfully tugged on his wooly ear. Looking back up, her smile withered. Mr. McDonald leaned against the white board fence, staring at her.

"Oh, Mr. McDonald. I didn't know you were...I'm taking Rocky to the..."

Mr. McDonald cleared his throat and moved closer. "I didn't mean to startle you." His gray eyes were sad. "I was watching...you remind me..." He stopped and took a breath, as if trying to find courage from within. "You remind me of Cindy when she was your age. Nyla thinks so, too. You have a good way with horses. Natural."

"Well...I...um...Thanks." Tara lowered her eyes, baffled by the compliment.

Mr. McDonald spoke again, his gruff voice faltering. "You probably know I didn't want you here. I don't need any more trouble."

Tara stayed silent. Afraid to say anything.

"I thought it was another one of Cindy's stubborn ideas to get back at me." He took a breath. "But she was right. Like that danged horse you saved—you deserved a second chance. You've got something...special."

Tara blinked. Special?

"Well, I need to get back to the house," Mr. McDonald rasped. "I sent Cindy's mom up there a bit ago. She wasn't feeling well."

Mr. McDonald turned to leave and stopped. Looking back he said sadly, "I know you've had a bum rap. I've talked with your social worker." He paused. "I had to know, since you're on my farm...wanted to know what we were getting into." His eyes misted. "I hope you don't hate your momma for the rest of your life...like Cindy does her dad."

Tara watched Mr. McDonald walk away. Her mind whirled. If he knew how Cindy felt, why didn't he do something?

Her thoughts drifted to her mother, her strained jaw and hollow eyes. Making a fist with one hand, a mix of emotions coursed through her, welling into the pit of her stomach. Her mother had left her. Ruined her life. How was she supposed to feel?

She let out a long breath, her hand relaxing. She wanted to hate her. But she didn't. She only wanted her love. Why couldn't her mother love her?

She blinked away a tear.

CHAPTER FIFTEEN

Tara stood on the edge of the porch, sunshine caressing her face, its warmth spreading throughout her body. The sweet aroma of Mrs. McDonald's rose garden wafted on the afternoon breeze. Tara watched her prune and fertilize the roses, the red blooms brilliant against the manicured lawn. She spent a lot of time caring for the flowers and it showed, earning compliments from everyone who visited Freedom Farms. Tara smiled, her thoughts drifting to the barn. Mrs. McDonald must love those roses as much as she loved Trouble.

Mrs. McDonald stretched and glanced up. Spying Tara, she waved a gloved hand. "Good morning Tara," she called. "It's so nice to see you."

Tara waved back, heading to the garden. "Hi, Mrs. McDonald. How are you? Are you feeling better?

"Oh my husband…" Mrs. McDonald groused, waving a hand at the house. "He's such a worry wart. You'd think I was made of glass the way he acts."

Tara smiled. "Your roses are sure pretty."

"Thank you. They mean a lot to me." Mrs. McDonald wiped the back of her glove across her forehead, gazing at the open blooms. She turned back to Tara. "Are you working with Trouble today? You're doing such a good job with him. Sam is so pleased."

Tara pushed her hair behind her ear. "I'm working him on the lunge line today. He likes to get out." A whinny sounded from the barn and she laughed. "There he is now. I think he's getting impatient. I better go get him out." She waved goodbye and hurried off.

* * * *

The lunge line bobbed in Tara's hand. Trouble cantered in a wide circle around her, the boards of the corral fence blurring as he galloped round and round. She watched his black legs stride, his muscles rippling under his glossy coat and his mane and tail streaming like black banners in the wind. He held his chiseled head high, eyes sparkling, nostrils flared. Tara smiled. Life couldn't get any better than this.

Mr. McDonald joined his wife at the rose garden and leaned in to kiss her cheek, before moving on toward the house. Tara watched their brief encounter, admiring the love they shared. Cindy was lucky to have such a wonderful mother.

As Trouble loped effortlessly around her, Tara's thoughts wavered to her own mother. Where was she? What was she doing? Was she ever coming back?

Could things have ever been different? Visions of a different life filled Tara's thoughts...her mother sitting on a porch swing with her, happy, laughing—the father she never knew leaning in to hug her and kiss the top of her head. A family.

Trouble tossed his head, enjoying the run. Tara jolted back to reality and scoffed. Dreams of a family were futile, a pipedream. Still, if only her mother would come back, she'd do anything to make her happy. Half a family would be better than no family.

"He's looking great," Sam called, leaning against the corral fence.

Tara turned and smiled broadly. She tugged on the line to stop Trouble and pulled him toward her. Sam waited for her by the fence and a tingle of excitement flowed to her fingertips. "I'm glad you're back. I've been working with him every day, just like you said. He's great. Hasn't acted up for me at all."

Sam's gaze moved over the horse.

Tara couldn't take it anymore and blurted out, "When can I ride him?" She waited, anxious, yet afraid of his answer.

Sam was quiet, his face thoughtful. "I don't want to rush anything. You were pretty lucky before. I'm still not certain we can trust him under the saddle."

"But, he hasn't…"

"I'm not saying you haven't done wonders gentling him. I just don't want to have him to get scared and go wild on us again."

Deep down Tara knew Sam was right…as usual. Even though she really wanted to ride him, it was more important to make sure Trouble knew nothing was going to hurt him.

"Why don't we try putting the saddle and bridle on him—see how he responds?"

Tara smiled, satisfied with the compromise.

Sam grinned. "Walk him around a little and cool him off. I'll get the saddle." He started for the barn then stopped for a moment. "I think we'll try a western saddle on him. He didn't seem to care for Alissa's fancy English one. "

Tara had seen Sam and some of the others riding with the western saddle. It was so much different with the saddle horn and longer stirrups. "Do you think it will make a difference?" Tara asked.

"Maybe. The one I want to use is much more relaxed than

Alissa's saddle. Hopefully he'll remember. It's what I started him on." He reached a hand out toward Trouble, a look of surprise crossing his face when Trouble didn't lay his ears back. "Trouble was such a nice horse when he first got here. I wish I knew what had caused him to change."

Tara knew. Alissa was what caused him to change.

"Well, let's try the western saddle and see what he does."

Tara walked Trouble around the corral, breathing in the earthy scents of the farm, her adoration for Trouble filling her as they walked side by side. Trouble nuzzled her hand and lipped at the lead rope. Turning his head, he watched Sam come back out of the barn, a western saddle in one hand, two bridles in the other. As Sam heaved the saddle onto the top board of the corral, Trouble snorted and danced to the side.

"Easy, boy, easy," Tara cooed.

Trouble stopped and stared at the saddle, his eyes rimmed with white.

Tara held the lead firm, stroking his cheek, talking quietly—reminding him nothing was ever going to hurt him again. Trouble calmed and leaned into Tara's hand. Sam inched over and rubbed a green saddle blanket over Trouble's strong neck and shoulders. He placed it over his red back and smoothed it out. Trouble quivered as he turned his head and sniffed at the blanket. Sam moved quietly back and retrieved the saddle, laying it on the ground by Trouble's front legs. Trouble shuddered and stepped back.

"It's okay," Tara whispered, tugging on Trouble's halter. He pulled back momentarily, then snorted at the leather flaps.

Sam slipped next to Tara, reaching for the lead rope. "I'll hold him and you try to put the saddle on his back. He trusts you. But if you see him so much as start to move, you get up on the fence, okay?"

Tara nodded and let Sam take the rope. She moved slow,

bending down to pick up the saddle, pausing to let Trouble sniff at the leather. She inched toward his back, talking softly, letting him watch her.

Up on the hill, Mrs. McDonald stopped pruning her roses and watched them.

"Easy, Trouble," she cooed. "You trust me, don't you?"

Trouble's ears pricked forward, waiting, watching.

Tara lifted the saddle. Trouble hunched his back as it touched. Tara waited, holding Trouble's gaze. He relaxed, letting out a long breath. His apprehension gone, Tara placed the saddle on Trouble's back, easing it down onto the blanket and grinned at Sam.

He nodded. "Go ahead. Cinch it."

Tara patted Trouble's shoulder and bent to reach the cinch and pull it around his middle, beaming with her accomplishment. Surely Sam had to see Trouble was okay with things and would let her ride.

The bridles clinked in the breeze from where they hung on the pole. Tara lifted the top bridle, feeling the cold metal bit in her hand. She turned to Trouble and lifted the bit to his mouth. Trouble pulled back and snorted wildly, his muscles taut and rigid.

"Whoa," Sam said, holding onto the lead rope, bracing himself in case the horse took off.

Tara frowned, her hopes dashed, sure Trouble was having visions of the painful bridle Alissa had forced him to wear, creating those terrible sores on his mouth.

"Tara, throw the bridle over the fence and show him you don't have it anymore."

Tara did as Sam instructed, holding empty hands up to Trouble. He relaxed again, shaking his long mane.

"Try the other one," Sam said. "It's a hackamore. Doesn't use a bit. I was afraid Trouble wouldn't take the bit." Sam pointed toward the other bridle. "Bring it over, but don't go near his mouth. I'll show you how it goes on."

Tara picked the second bridle up, fingering the strange noseband.

Sam pointed to the stiff leather arc. "This uses pressure points on the nose to control the horse. See if Trouble will let you put it on."

Tara stepped toward Trouble, holding the strange bridle out for him to sniff. He grunted, stretching his neck, staying where he stood. She eased the noseband over his black muzzle, reaching up to put the crown piece over his ears. Trouble's ears flickered offering no further resistance.

Sam grunted. "If I'd been a betting man, I would have lost a ton of money today. Trouble really trusts you."

Tara grinned and rubbed Trouble's cheek. "Yeah, I guess he does."

"Walk him around and see how he reacts to the saddle as he moves."

Tara barely felt her feet touch the ground as she led Trouble around the corral.

"I never thought I'd see a saddle on him again," Cindy said, walking up to Sam on a tall buckskin.

Trouble turned his head and nickered. Tara waved and finished the circle, directing Trouble to the corral fence next to her. He touched noses with the buckskin between the boards.

"So where you off to Cindy?" Sam asked.

Cindy nodded down the dirt road winding past the barns and over the hill. "It's such a beautiful day. I'm taking Buck here out to check on the new colts in the south pasture."

A twang of jealousy tugged at Tara, wishing she could go with her...on Trouble.

Cindy waved and galloped down the dusty road.

The late afternoon sun shimmered on the white barn,

stretching dark shadows on the ground. Tara circled Trouble on the lunge line again as Sam hooted with delight. Trouble loped easily, seeming not to care one bit about the weight upon his back or the strange bridle on his head. At Sam's command, Tara stopped Trouble and pulled him to her, wondering if it was possible to die from too much happiness.

Mrs. McDonald waved and smiled from her rose bed, clapping her encouragement.

"You've got a fan," Tara purred to Trouble, rubbing his shoulder. "See?" Tara gazed back up the hill. Mrs. McDonald's smile drooped off her face as she waved a hand in front of her flushed face. She took a step and crumpled to the grass next to the roses.

"Mrs. McDonald!" Tara yelled and leaped at the fence, crawling over the boards like a monkey. Trouble startled and trotted a few feet away, turning around to gaze after her.

"What are you doing?" Sam yelled after her.

"Cindy's mom. Something's wrong!" She pointed to where Mrs. McDonald lay.

Tara raced up the hill to the rose bed. She could hear Sam fling the gate to the corral open and his footsteps pounded behind her, quickly catching up with her. Mrs. McDonald lay unconscious in the grass. Sam bent over her, checking her pulse and patting her hand. "Nyla? Wake up, Nyla."

With a grave nod to Tara, he pressed his hands to her chest, pumping a rhythm for her heart. Richard appeared in the door of the barn and Sam shouted for him to fetch Mr. McDonald from the house. Tara couldn't breathe, the air held captive in her chest, the memory of Grandma Kay ping-ponging in her head.

Sam leaned in momentarily. "Nyla? Come on, Nyla."

No response. He continued his compressions.

Richard pounded on the door of the big house, yelling for Mr. McDonald. The door opened and he pointed to where Sam knelt on the ground. Tara could hear Richard's voice rise as his arms gestured toward them. "It's her and that horse...I told you...they're trouble..."

Tara gazed to where Richard now pointed, eyes wide as she spied Trouble standing not ten feet away, watching her. Trouble was out of the corral? Her eyes darted to the open gate, swinging wide.

Mr. McDonald rushed down the hill, his partially buttoned shirt ruffling behind him while Richard disappeared into the house, reappearing with a phone to his ear.

"What have you done?" Mr. McDonald pushed Tara back and dropped to the ground beside his wife. "Nyla? Honey?" His voice strangled as he called to her. He glared up at Trouble, his icy stare then turning to Tara. "What'd you do to her?"

Tara stood and took a shaky step backward. Her eyes filled with tears. "I didn't do anything. I saw her...and we...we ran..." Why did he think it was her fault? She didn't do anything. She'd never hurt Mrs. McDonald.

"Tara," Sam said, his voice barely loud enough to hear, continuing his rhythmic compressions. "Go...find...Cindy."

Mr. McDonald bent over his wife, crying. Tara nodded to Sam, choking back her own fears. She knew where the south pasture was. It was way too far to run on foot and it would take too long to saddle another horse.

Trouble nickered, pawing at the grass, the lunge line trailing behind him. Sam would be mad, but there was nothing else to do. This was an emergency.

With a quick flip of her hands, Tara unhooked the lunge line and grabbed Trouble's reins. Placing a foot to the stirrup, she lifted herself up and swung her leg over Trouble's back, holding her breath and praying he trusted her. So far so good. Crouching low in the saddle, she urged him down the dirt path leading to the pasture.

"Come on Trouble," she whispered. "Go!"

Trouble hurtled down the lane, mane streaming into Tara's face. She clung to his back, her brown ponytail whipping behind her as they streaked away.

CHAPTER SIXTEEN

Tara gripped Trouble's sides with her legs as they sped down the dirt road. The horse's powerful muscles rippled, strong and supple beneath her. His black-tipped ears lay flat against his head, his stride lengthening as he ran.

Tara's hands tingled. She was riding Trouble. Riding him without so much as a buck or balk. He trusted her.

Though happy Trouble trusted her, her joy of riding him was clouded with dark worries. Would Mrs. McDonald be okay? Would Sam take Trouble away from her for her disobedience? Would Mr. McDonald send her back to the Bonner Home for misfits?

She clutched the reins as Sam had shown her last week, watching Trouble's dark legs propel them forward. The wind stung her face, forcing her to narrow her eyes, tears streaming back into her hair. Fence posts blurred past as Trouble's hooves drummed in her ears like the steady rhythm of a locomotive. They had to find Cindy!

"We're almost there," Tara yelled. "I see the gate."

She reined Trouble to a prancing stop next to the gate. Without dismounting, she lifted the catch and eased the anxious horse through, fastening it behind her. Trouble needed only to be pointed toward a rise in the pasture and without further encouragement, took off at a gallop, covering the ground as fast as the wind. A small group of mares and foals ran ahead of them, scattering before stopping and turning back to stare at the horse and rider.

"There she is," Tara shouted to his quivering ears. She pressed the reins against Trouble's neck and raced toward the buckskin horse in the distance.

Buck whinnied, his head high, looking in Tara's direction. Cindy appeared from behind him and raised a hand to shade her eyes. Tara waved wildly as she pressed Trouble on.

"Cindy! It's your mom..."

Cindy stiffened.

Tara pulled back on the reins, tugging Trouble to a bouncy stop. "It's your mom, Cindy. Something's wrong. You have to get back to the house. *Now!*"

Cindy jumped into Buck's saddle and took off toward the farm. Trouble tugged at the reins, ready to race after her but Tara held him steady. She needed to cool him down first. "Whoa, boy," she said softly, stroking his sweating neck. Cindy had expressed how important it was to not let them get overheated. "Easy. We'll take it a little slower going back."

Tara eased Trouble into a slow trot and followed Cindy's tracks. Trouble snorted, blowing out a long breath. His ears flickered, his head and tail high, an excited glimmer in his eyes. Tara wasn't excited. She was in no hurry to get back to the farm and face the trouble she knew she'd be in. Sam told her not to ride Trouble and she did. He'd probably never let her ride him again. She'd be lucky if he'd ever let her even get close to him again.

Her eyes misted over.

That was if she was even allowed to stay at the farm. For some reason, Mr. McDonald blamed her for his wife's fall. She'd seen that look before. It wouldn't do any good to tell him otherwise. He wouldn't believe her.

* * * *

Tara trotted Trouble along the dusty lane as the ambulance screamed down the highway and turned into the farm's drive. Cindy huddled close to Sam as he continued CPR on Mrs. McDonald.

"Over here," Mr. McDonald yelled at the ambulance, motioning them onto the grass.

Two EMTs jumped out and took over the compressions from Sam. A third man pulled a gurney from the vehicle.

"You've got to save her," Mr. McDonald bellowed at the second EMT.

Sam wrapped an arm around Cindy as she sobbed into his shoulder. He glanced up, his face lined, eyes dark. Tara swallowed. Yup. He was mad. No, he was furious.

Tara hung her head, biting back the tears threatening to fall.

Buck stood at the far end of the corral, still wearing the saddle and bridle, watching the red lights of the ambulance with white-rimmed eyes. Tara led Trouble into the corral with him and unsaddled both horses, rubbing their sweaty bodies down, all the while watching the activity by the rose garden.

The technicians bundled Mrs. McDonald on the gurney and carried her to the ambulance. Cindy jumped in the back with her. Sam led Mr. McDonald to the driveway where Richard waited with a long black car. After helping Mr. McDonald into the passenger side, Sam dashed around to the other side, standing face to face with Richard, motioning down the hill to Tara. She could only guess what they were saying, sure it wasn't anything good. Heated voices exchanged words and Sam jumped into the driver's seat. In a flash they were all gone—Mrs. McDonald, Mr. McDonald, Sam, and Cindy. Left alone in the driveway, Richard glared down the hill at her, then turned and stalked off into the east barn.

Tara watched the dust settle from the vehicles, fighting the urge to throw up, her world crumbling around her. She leaned against the fence, blinking tears back. She'd never been happy before coming to Freedom Farms. And now she'd ruined it all.

Trouble turned his head, wrapping Tara in a horse hug. Tara grabbed hold of his neck and let the sobs rock out of her, tears flowing down her face and mingling with the dried sweat on Trouble's neck. Finally, she leaned back and gazed into his big brown eyes.

"You've proven them wrong, Trouble." She smiled, her eyes glazed over. "You've shown them you're the best horse ever." She hung her head. "Me? Trouble seems to follow me everywhere I go." She leaned in, half-laughing at the unintended pun, feeling the warmth of his horse body. "I wish you could follow me everywhere." A single tear slipped down her face. "I can't do anything right."

Tara finished caring for the horses, trying to keep her mind occupied. After putting them in their stalls and giving them extra rations of oats and water, she cleaned the tack, taking care to not only soap the leather, but to condition it as well.

It was long after dinnertime and Tara's stomach growled, though the mere thought of food made her want to throw up again. She headed back to Cindy's, creeping through the shadowed farm yard. Cindy's empty house stood dark and gloomy. Tara trudged through the small front room and hallway, not bothering to turn on the lights. If there was no light, no one could witness the swollen eyes and red nose she was sure she wore, like a scarlet letter of shame. Though there was no one to see them anyway.

In her bedroom, Tara turned on the small lamp by her bed, boxing up her meager belongings in the dim light of the one bulb and stacking the two boxes by the door. She sat on the bed and waited, her body and mind weary. Shadows played over the picture on the wall, the black horse suspended in midair, the jump well beneath its shiny hooves tucked so elegantly underneath. So, this had been Cindy's dream. An ache burned in Tara's heart. Don't give up on your dream. That's what Cindy had said. But the only dream that mattered to her was to be around Trouble. He loved and accepted her, like the family she longed for. And now her dream was dying, just like she was dying inside.

Tara turned off the lamp, sitting in the darkness. A whinny floated through the open window from the pasture beside the barn. Tara didn't move, continuing to stare at the wall. A car slowed on the highway and the sound of crunching gravel mixed with the horse voices as the vehicle pulled up the lane. Car lights flashed momentarily in her window and headed up to the house on the hill. Under the tall yard light, Tara watched Sam get out. Richard met him. They talked briefly. Richard nodded and went into the house while Sam headed down toward Cindy's. Tara held her breath. This was it.

A knock sounded on the screen door. It creaked as it opened and clicked shut. Steps headed down the hall.

"Tara?" Sam asked, flipping on her overhead light. "What are you doing here in the dark?"

Tara blinked and stood up, wishing her hair wasn't tied in a ponytail. No way to hide her tell-tale swollen eyes now. "How's Mrs. McDonald?" Her voice cracked. "Is she going to be okay?"

Sam took a breath. "She had a heart attack. Thanks to you, though, she got the help she needed right away." He stopped and gazed at her two small boxes. "What's this? You going somewhere?"

Tara looked down at the floor, staring at the patterned rug. "I figured I'd be ready. I know I'm in trouble."

Sam tilted his head. "Trouble?" He raised an eyebrow. "Oh...because you rode Trouble after I told you not to?"

Tara didn't respond, wishing he wouldn't make this any harder than it already was.

Sam leaned in and put an arm around her. "On the contrary, I think it was very brave of you."

Tara looked up at him. "But you looked so mad at me. And you left without saying anything. I thought..."

"Mad at you? I wasn't mad at you. I was mad at Richard. Didn't he tell you I'd be back? I told him to leave you a note and keep an eye on you."

Tara shook her head. "I haven't seen any note."

Sam's brows furrowed, anger pursing his lips. "Just one more thing I will have to talk to Richard about."

Tara drew a quick breath, her next question burning on her tongue. "You aren't going to send me away?"

Sam's face softened and he put a leathery hand on Tara's arm. "No one is going to send you away, Tara. Who would take care of Trouble if you left?" He grinned, attempting to lure a smile from her in return. She tried, giving him a small one-sided smile.

Sam continued. "Do you know the real reason I didn't want you to ride Trouble? I was afraid of what he would do to *you* if you got on him again. I didn't want anything to happen to you. That didn't stop you though. Your first thought today was for Cindy and you took a chance Trouble's trust would keep him from hurting you. You proved it would."

Tara stared at Sam in disbelief. "So you're not mad at me?"

Sam shook his head.

Tara let out a heavy sigh. "Well, Mr. McDonald sure is. He blames me and Trouble for what happened to Cindy's mom. You know I didn't. I didn't touch her. I'd never…"

"I know," Sam said and put a hand up to quiet her. "He's just upset. Richard saw Trouble loose and jumped to conclusions. Don't worry. I'm sure we'll get it straightened out.

"Cindy and her dad are staying at the hospital. Cindy's brother joined them there. I'll stay here with you tonight." He looked down the hallway. "I'll sleep on the couch."

Tara leaned back on the bed, all of the sudden tired and worn out, the knot in her shoulders relaxing now that she knew Sam wasn't going to separate her from Trouble. She only hoped Mrs. McDonald was going to be okay too.

Sam walked over to the window and stared out toward the pasture. "You know, I never knew Trouble had that kind of speed in him."

"Speed?"

Sam turned to look at her. "Yeah. Trouble lit out of here like his tail was on fire. I don't know if I've ever seen a horse move so fast."

"Really?" She looked out the window, remembering the ride, feeling the wind on her face, Trouble's power beneath her. "I guess he knew it was important."

"Maybe." He slipped out the bedroom door and then stuck his head back in and asked, "Want to ride him again tomorrow?"

Tara's stomach flip-flopped. Unable to control her excitement, she bounced up off the bed and hugged Sam's neck. "Oh, sorry." She blushed and pulled back, peering up at Sam. "I didn't mean to get all gushy."

Sam laughed. "Well, I would have been disappointed if you hadn't shown some kind of enthusiasm. After all, you don't get asked to ride the horse called Trouble every day. You're the best thing that ever happened to him."

Tara smiled, her insides exploding in happiness. Sam had it all wrong. He was the best thing that ever happened to her.

CHAPTER SEVENTEEN

The morning sun rose high in the sky before Tara was able to leave the house in search of Sam, the screen door rattling in her flurry.

"Why did Cindy *have* to remember the stupid history project," she grumbled to herself, thinking back to Cindy's early morning phone call. Tara was glad to hear the report that Mrs. McDonald was better, but she could have done without Cindy remembering the project. She'd have rather been with Trouble. Especially since Sam told her she could ride him today.

Tara wandered through the barn and found Sam putting fresh straw in a large stall.

"I'm all done with my history," she said, peering over the half-door.

Sam leaned on his pitchfork. "Good. Miss Elizabeth will pick it up this afternoon."

A dark foal stretched his neck and nibbled at the red and white handkerchief sticking out of Sam's back pocket. He tugged at the fabric and jumped back as it popped free and floated to the straw.

Tara grinned. "That's Moonbeam, isn't it? He's really growing."

Sam nodded as Moonbeam pranced around the side of the black mare and reared at her head. The mare laid her ears back and turned away, swishing her tail, giving the colt her motherly warning. "He's getting a little rambunctious. They'll be turned out to pasture pretty soon. I think momma here will be pretty happy about that."

Tara laughed as the frisky colt head-butted the side of his mother.

Sam leaned against the pitchfork. "I found Richard's note last night. Not sure how you missed it. He put it right on the table as you walked in the house."

Tara chewed on the side of her lip. "It was dark when I went in the house and I never turned on the lights."

"Yeah, I wondered." He bent down to retrieve his handkerchief. "Richard still should have made sure you knew what was going on. I think you intimidate him."

"Me?" Tara startled.

"Yes, you." Sam grinned. "Why don't you get Trouble saddled and I'll meet you at the corral. We'll work with him and give you a riding lesson at the same time."

Tara floated on air as she waltzed down the aisle. Trouble nickered a friendly hello. She wrapped her arms around his neck, feeling the love pour from her heart.

Outside the barn, a red-haired girl trotted her sorrel horse in circles. Tara held Trouble close, watching the horse in the corral prance, muscle taut, his eyes darting to the barrels in the arena. Sweat coated his neck and hips, his sides heaving. "One more run, Red," the girl called and leaned forward, pressing the horse into a full run toward the first metal drum. She reined the horse around it and charged toward a second barrel on the other side of the corral. Circling that one, she raced toward a third barrel at the far end.

Tara watched in amazement as the girl and horse flew through the cloverleaf pattern, the horse's mane and tail whipping, muscles pumping.

Around the third barrel, the girl cheered her horse on even faster, back to the beginning of the pattern. She pulled him to a stop, patting his neck and cooing words of encouragement as she trotted around the end of the arena.

"All ready, Tara?" Sam asked as he walked up and put an elbow on the top board of the corral.

"Hi Sam," the red-haired girl called.

"Hi Janie, how's Red's time?"

Janie pulled the sorrel to a stop next to the fence and patted his shoulder. "He's doing great. We're just about done for today if you need the corral. Want to cool him off with one more round."

Tara watched the girl trot the horse slowly around the barrels again, tracing the pattern she'd just run. "What's she doing?"

"Janie?" Sam gazed at the girl. "She's practicing. Her horse, Red, is one of the top barrel racers in the state. It's a gymkhana event at horse shows." He pointed to the three barrels. "The rider runs his horse around the barrels in a cloverleaf fashion and you race against the clock. Best time wins."

Tara nodded. "Looks kind of fun."

Janie rode to the end of the corral and hopped off her horse.

"Janie's good," Sam said, matter-of-factly. "She's won lots of trophies. Though, after seeing Trouble run yesterday, I think he could give Red a run for his money."

Tara sputtered. Trouble? A barrel horse? "Do you really think Trouble is fast?"

Sam smiled, a teasing gleam in his eye. "You interested?"

Tara bit her lip. "Well, maybe. I guess so. It looks fun and if you think Trouble could do it."

Janie led her horse out of the arena to the water trough.

Sam reached over and patted Trouble's face. "Well, let's not rush it. We'll see how he does today. Maybe we can try it sometime and see if he's as good as I think he is."

For the next hour, Tara followed Sam's instructions. Walk, trot, canter. Turn, walk, trot, canter. Trouble performed perfectly. Tara beamed as she sat in the western saddle, feeling Trouble move beneath her. She couldn't get Sam's words out of her mind. Trouble was faster than Red. And Red was a champion barrel horse. Could she teach Trouble to do it? She'd love to try and prove to everyone what kind of horse Trouble really was.

A car door slammed and Cindy's blonde head bobbed above the other side of the car. Tara reined Trouble toward the fence next to Sam, anxious for an update on Mrs. McDonald. One look at Cindy's face, though, told her things weren't so good. Was it her Mom? Or was it something else? Cindy stormed toward the corral, angry eyes focused on the ground in front of her.

A second car pulled up behind Cindy's and a man got out and ran after her. Tara knew in an instant it must be her brother, Jake. He had the same facial features and blond hair as Cindy.

"Cindy," the man said gruffly. "Will you just listen to me?"

Cindy turned stiffly to face him. "No, Jake, I won't listen to you. Dad's such a jerk…like always. How could he believe Richard and even think Tara and Trouble were to blame for Mom's heart attack? They couldn't have done anything to cause it. And Richard…Richard's as gullible as a six year-old if he believes anything Alissa Jordan tells him. Tara is not a trouble-maker."

Tara listened in stunned silence.

Trouble snorted and Cindy jumped. Turning, she looked surprised to see Tara and Trouble. Her face softened, but her eyes still smoldered. "I'm sorry you heard that, Tara. I know you didn't have anything to do with Mom's condition." Cindy faced her brother again. "I'll go back up and see Mom later...when Dad is *not* there. I don't know how she stayed with him all this time."

"Cindy," Jake argued. "Dad's upset. You know how he gets when he's upset. He talks without thinking. Please go back with me so we can straighten this out."

"Well, upset or not, I don't want to be in the same room with him. Not after everything he's done."

"What's he done? I mean, I know you two never got along when we were kids, but we're adults now. You're not making any sense." Jake shook his head and let out an exasperated sigh.

"I couldn't ever do anything to please him." Cindy slapped her fist against her leg. "So I wasn't as good in school as you were? So I got in trouble all the time? So what? It didn't give him the right to..." She bit at her lip and said with force. "I'll never forgive him for what he did to Jupiter."

Jake's mouth fell open. "Is that what you've been upset over all these years? You're still mad about that stupid horse?"

Tara gulped in surprise. How could he say that? Jupiter had been Cindy's best friend. Tara slipped out of the saddle and stood by the fence, facing Jake. "He was more than a horse to Cindy. He meant everything to her." She put a trembling hand on Trouble's shoulder. She knew exactly how Cindy felt.

Jake scowled at Tara. "I don't think this concerns you, Miss."

Cindy spouted back, hands clenched. "It does concern Tara. She's the one Dad and Richard so wickedly accused. *And* if anyone knows how I feel, it's her."

Tara slid an arm around Trouble's neck, laying her head against his warm skin.

Cindy raised a fist at Jake. "And yes, I'm still mad. I'm *furious!*

Dad killed my best friend."

Jake stepped back. "What? Who told you he was dead?"

"No one *told* me." Cindy spat. "I figured it out myself. It didn't take much to put two and two together. Stonewall buying up all the horses and then my horse disappears. I knew all along Dad sold Jupiter to him. Stonewall killed him!"

Jake stood silent, his face turning ashen. He glanced at Tara and Sam. Looking back to Cindy, he began to speak, his voice hushed and pained. "It's not what you think, Cindy. It's not like that at all." His shoulders drooped. "You don't know the whole story. You need to know the truth."

CHAPTER EIGHTEEN

Cindy stared at her brother. "What do you mean, Jake? What truth?"

Jake stared at the ground.

Tara held her breath, unable to move, afraid if she did, she'd miss it all. What could this truth be?

Cindy placed her hands on her waist and glared at Jake. Trouble snorted, breaking the silence.

"Well?" Cindy rumbled. "Why did Dad sell Jupiter to Stonewall…to let him be slaughtered?"

Jake grimaced. "Dad didn't sell Jupiter to Stonewall."

Cindy leaned in. "He didn't? Well if he didn't, who'd he sell him to?" A slight glimmer of hope shone from her eyes.

Tara knew what Cindy was thinking. If Jupiter was still alive, maybe she could find him and get him back.

Jake remained silent. Cindy kept pressing. "Just because I was in trouble at school, it still didn't give Dad the right to sell Jupiter to anyone. He was *my* horse!"

Tears welled in Jake's eyes. "Dad didn't sell him, Cin."

Tara wound her fingers nervously into Trouble's mane.

Cindy's eyes flashed. "What? Of course he did. He *told* me he sold him."

"I know what Dad told you," Jake said quietly. "And he made us promise to never tell you the truth. He said time would pass and you'd get over it." He swallowed. "I guess you never did."

"He said I'd get over it?" Cindy's face flushed. "How could I get over losing my best friend? How was I supposed to get over losing my dream?"

Trouble stomped his hoof and shook his head, pulling his mane free from Tara's fingers. She couldn't imagine someone trying to tell her to forget Trouble. She couldn't even forget about Homer and he'd found a good home.

Jake took a deep breath. "I guess Dad hoped you would forget. We all did."

Cindy shook her head, her blond ponytail swinging. "Well, I didn't."

Sam put his hand on Cindy's shoulder and said softly, "Why don't you two go inside where you can have some privacy."

Cindy frowned, snapping back at Sam. "I don't need privacy." She fixed her stare back on Jake. "If he knows what happened to Jupiter, I want to know…right now."

Jake's shoulders slumped forward. He looked at his hands, twisting his college class ring. "You were at the National Convention for school. Mom and Dad were so glad you'd decided to go. Dad thought maybe you were finally taking more of an interest in school."

Cindy huffed. "I didn't go to the conference because of school. I knew a girl who rode jumpers back east was going to be there. I wanted to find out who her trainer was. She hooked me up and I was going to take Jupiter out there after graduation."

Jake let out a long breath, his mouth quivering. "Oh, man.

Did Dad ever know?"

"No," Cindy's jaw twitched. "Why would I share that with him? After all, he's the one who destroyed my dream."

"Dad didn't do it." Jake groaned. "Mom and I did."

Tara shot a look at Sam, who, looking back at her, mirrored her surprise.

"What do you mean?" Cindy croaked. "What did you do with Jupiter? Where is he?"

Jake's face went pale as he continued twisting his ring. "Mom went out to take care of Jupiter after you left. You know she loved Jupiter almost as much as you did. She put him in the corral so he could stretch his legs a little. There'd been this big German Shepherd running loose and Mom tried chasing him away.

"I was late for basketball practice and kept yelling at her to hurry up. I guess she didn't get the gate latched all the way.

"Mom and I were headed to the car when we heard it."

Cindy leaned toward Jake. Her voice wavered. "Heard what?"

Jake looked up at Cindy. Tears streaked his face. "Jupiter got out and the dog chased him. Chased him out down the driveway. Jupiter ran out on the highway and a semi hit him."

Cindy cried out and stepped back. Sam caught her arm to keep her from falling.

Jake took a breath. "Dad heard Jupiter scream and ran out there, but there wasn't anything he could do. The impact broke both of Jupiter's back legs."

Tears flowed down Cindy's face as she leaned against Sam, her face ghostly white.

"Dad did the only thing he could. He put Jupiter out of his misery. He hated it and bawled like a baby all night."

Cindy turned and hid her face in Sam's shoulder, her body shaking as she sobbed.

"I'm so sorry, Cindy," Jake said softly. "It's all my fault. If I hadn't hurried Mom...Mom felt horrible. She was afraid you'd never forgive her. So Dad decided to tell you he sold him. Mom argued, but he said you were already mad at him anyway. Said you'd get over it eventually. He didn't want you to get mad at Mom. She was already a nervous wreck with everything the way it was."

"How could Dad think I wouldn't forgive her?"

Jake shook her head. "Would you have? You were always mad back then. I didn't think you would either. At least not right away. And it would have killed Mom."

It was Cindy's turn to be silent. A silence so thick Tara thought she might suffocate. Finally Cindy turned to stare at Jake again. "So what did Dad do with Jupiter?" Bitterness seeped back into her voice. "Did he send him off to the rendering plant? Is that all my horse meant to anyone?"

Jake shook his head and stared up toward the big house again. "Dad didn't ship his body anywhere. He laid Jupiter to rest in the yard. He and Mom, both, insisted on a special place for him. Weren't you surprised to come back and see a rose garden planted so early in the season? It was barely warm enough to plant anything."

Tara looked up at the rose bed, her eyes misting.

Cindy's eyes followed Tara's gaze. "You mean, Jupiter's under there?"

Jake nodded. "Why do you think Mom tends those roses like she does? It's her way of paying tribute to Jupiter."

Cindy whimpered. "So why didn't Dad ever tell me?"

"Mom wanted to," Jake croaked. "She was beside herself with guilt. Dad wouldn't let us tell you. He was afraid of what it would do to Mom if you got as upset with her as you are with him. After you took off, we didn't see you for a long time. And when we did, you never mentioned Jupiter again and...I guess we all thought you'd moved on with it."

Cindy looked to Sam. "Who else knew?"

Jake shook his head. "Sam wasn't here yet. Richard helped Dad bury Jupiter, but he was sworn to secrecy."

Cindy stared from the corral to the roses to the barn. She choked back a sob. "I need to be alone. I have to sort this out." She staggered to the barn entrance and disappeared into the shadows.

Tara gazed at the rose garden. The flowers raised their fragrant blossoms to the sun, their aroma wafting on the breeze. She sniffed as a tear rolled down her cheek, imagining Cindy's horse, never to jump again, lying under the memorial of flowers. Jake was right when he said their mother loved Jupiter. Tara could almost see her there, tending the roses, her hands caressing the stems as though they were precious china, showering the garden with love and affection...to remember him.

Sam interrupted her thoughts, his voice hushed. "Why don't you put Trouble in his stall now? Give him an extra ration of grain. He deserves it."

Tara nodded and led Trouble toward the barn as the two men walked slowly toward the big house, their voices quiet and low. Trouble nuzzled her hand and she wrapped her arm around his nose, feeling the velvety soft muzzle against her skin.

"I can imagine how Cindy must feel." She stared into Trouble's dark eyes. "I'd want to die if I found out something like that happened to you."

She pressed her face against Trouble's silky cheek. Closing her eyes, she breathed in the smells of the farm, the hay and leather and horse sweat, feeling her body relax with the horse's warm flesh and rhythmic breathing. She released her hold and led him inside.

Tara went through the routine of stripping the saddle and bridle off Trouble, brushing him down, giving him his grain…but her mind wasn't on it. All she could think of was Cindy. How she must feel. Jupiter was dead. Mr. McDonald hadn't done it. Not like Cindy thought, anyway. He'd lied to her. But he'd lied to protect Mrs. McDonald.

How could he think Cindy would forget Jupiter, though? She couldn't.

"Tara?" A voice spoke quietly behind her.

Tara turned. "Cindy. Are you okay? I'm so sorry." Tears fell again. She couldn't help it.

Cindy nodded and tried to smile. "Thanks."

"It's awful. I can only imagine how you…I don't know what I'd do if…" Tara stared at Trouble.

"I know."

"So are you going back to the hospital to talk to your dad now?"

Cindy's cheeks reddened. "No. I'm still trying to understand it all. He lied to me. He told me he *sold* Jupiter."

Tara bit her lip, remembering how sad Mr. McDonald had been when he talked about Cindy being mad at her "old man." "I think you should talk to him, Cindy. He lied so you wouldn't be mad at your mom." She paused. "I think he deserves a second chance."

A frown creased Cindy's forehead. "You can say that, even after he blamed you for hurting my mom?"

Tara lowered her shoulders, raising her chin. "Well, I didn't. And you and Sam know I didn't." She brushed a stray lock of hair out of her eyes, surprised with her new found confidence. "Right or wrong…" She took a small breath, her voice lowering to almost a whisper. "He loves you. He told me." Tara gazed down at the straw, trying to mask the pain she knew welled in her eyes. "I wish I had a dad who loved me like that. My dad didn't even want to know me."

Turning, she brushed Trouble's back, long hard strokes, each pop of the brush trying to expel the sadness in her own heart. She *would* give anything to have a mom or dad who cared.

CHAPTER NINETEEN

Tara slipped her jeans on as the morning sun peeked through the window, the sound of pots and pans banging in the kitchen. Sam must be up. A half-smile crossed her face as she pictured him, wrinkled clothes and messy hair, fumbling with the coffee pot. With Cindy back at the hospital, it made her happy knowing he was there, camped out on the couch. He was kind of like the father she'd never had.

Sadness wrangled with Tara's heart, wishing she could have talked to Cindy. But by the time she'd finished brushing Trouble, Cindy was gone. Would she give her dad a second chance? He really did love her.

The strong smell of coffee drifted under the door.

Tara tugged on her boots and stood up to look in the mirror. Sorrow circled her green eyes, yet there was something else there, too…something that hadn't been there six weeks ago. She thought back to the person she'd been when she first arrived at Freedom Farms…a loner, afraid, with no family or friends. All that had changed. Except the family part anyway. Now, though, she had friends. She had people who cared. And she had Trouble.

Her brush swept through her hair, smoothing the brown strands as she pushed it off her face and into a ponytail holder. Turning, she moved to make her bed, and with a final pat on the bed spread, reached for the stuffed pony on the floor nearby. Fingering its fuzzy mane, lost in thought, she wished her mom loved her the same way as Cindy's mom and dad. Mr. McDonald was right. She didn't hate her mother. She'd do anything to give her a second chance.

Tossing the pony on the bed, she headed to the kitchen, only to stop and stare at the person standing at the stove.

"Good morning," Cindy called. "Sorry I wasn't here last night when you went to bed. I went back up to the hospital."

Tara's heart quickened. "You did? Is your mom okay? Did something happen?"

Cindy lifted a hand to her mouth and yawned. "No. Mom's doing much, much better." She pulled a mug from the cupboard. "I wanted to see her…and talk to my dad." She peeked over her shoulder at Tara.

"What? You talked to him? You were so…I thought you were mad at me."

Cindy poured coffee in her cup. "I'm not saying my dad and I are best friends, yet. But we've opened the door." She gazed out the window, a far-away look in her eyes. "I've been carrying around the pain of losing Jupiter for a long time. Keeping that anger locked in my heart only made the hurt worse, for me and everyone else. You made me realize that." She looked at Tara, her eyes moist. "I can't forget about Jupiter. He was more than just another horse to me. Dad's trying to understand that. He didn't have a clue that I'd made all those plans to show Jupiter and train jumpers. When I told him I'd re-contacted Scarborough Farms regarding a training position, he said he would give me a glowing reference."

A tear trickled down Cindy's face. "You were right, Tara, my dad does love me. He may not show it the way I want him to sometimes, but I guess he does love me." She sniffed. "He cried when I came back. And he gave me the biggest hug I've ever gotten from him. Mom was awake and she cried too, watching us."

Tara swallowed, stifling her own tears. She was happy she'd helped Cindy. At the same time, a twinge of jealousy filled her heart. Where was her fairy-tale ending?

Cindy sipped her coffee. "Well, you better go get your chores done before class. It's your last group session today."

Tara nodded. "It's sad. I've gotten to know all the kids. I'm really going to miss them, especially Simone. I've never had a real friend before."

Cindy smiled. "Well, you'll have to invite her out to ride this summer. Do you think she'd like that?"

Tara's face brightened. "She'd love it. You mean it? Can I ask her?"

Cindy laughed. "Sure." She pointed to the door. "Now go, so I can get dressed." Cindy sipped her coffee. "Oh," she pushed the cutting board on the counter toward Tara. "I cut some carrots for Trouble."

"Thanks." Tara grinned and grabbed a handful of carrot slices before dashing out the door.

Trouble nickered as she carried a bucket of water to his stall. He hung his head over the half door, eyes shining, nose reaching for her pockets.

"Hey, boy. How you doing this morning?" She set the bucket on the ground and took his head in her arms, hugging him close. "It's going to be a great day. Sam's meeting us later to give us some pointers on running the barrels. It's going to be so great."

Trouble nosed her pocket, obviously more interested in carrots than discussing barrels. Tara laughed.

"You're such a mooch."

She pulled out the carrots and offered them to him. "You are definitely *not* the same horse I saw the first day I got here. Where did Trouble go?"

Trouble snorted and stomped his hoof.

"Can I talk to you Tara?"

Tara turned to find Mr. McDonald standing in the aisle, hand on his hips.

"Oh, hi, Mr. McDonald. I didn't hear you come up. Sure, yeah. We can talk. Do you need something?" She forced her mouth to close, chastising herself silently. Sometimes she wished her tongue could revert to the old Tara.

Mr. McDonald's lips trembled. "I want to apologize, Tara." He pulled a white handkerchief out of his pocket and dabbed at his eye. "I was down-right nasty to you the other day. Thinking you'd done something to Nyla…"

"I'd never do anything to hurt her," Tara rushed.

Mr. McDonald nodded. "I know. I was stupid. I should have known better. You're a good girl. Nyla always said you were a good girl. If it hadn't been for you, Nyla could have laid there for a long time. She could have…" He turned his head, blinking rapidly.

"I'm glad I was there. And I'm so happy to hear she's doing better."

Mr. McDonald smiled. "Yes, and so are Cindy and I. I understand I have you to thank."

A blush rose to Tara's face.

Mr. McDonald smiled and took her hand in his. "Well, I just wanted to tell you I'm glad you're here." He sniffed and let go, stuffing the handkerchief back in his pocket. "I better go now. I need to do a few things around the farm before I head back to the hospital."

Tara watched him leave, a broad smile spreading across her face. She patted Trouble one last time and headed to the main barn to get the therapy horses ready for class. Rocky raised his head as she approached, his ears pricked forward. Tara laughed, thinking back to his grumpy attitude when she first met him.

"You're a changed horse, Rocky. You and Trouble both," she said as she scratched his fuzzy ears. "Seems there's been a lot of change going on around here."

"Hi Tara," Simone yelled and waved from the end of the aisle. Philly and Brandy waved and turned into the break room. Simone rushed down the corridor, her arms open, embracing Tara in a giant hug.

Happiness swirled inside and a smile lifted her mouth as she leaned it to accept the embrace. "Can you believe it's our last class today?" she asked, pulling away.

"I know. I'm going to really miss the horses." Simone grinned. "I never ever dreamt I'd say that. Me and horses? Go figure."

"Well...maybe you won't have to miss them for too long," Tara teased.

"What do you mean?"

Tara patted Rocky's neck. "Would you want to come out and visit me here this summer? Cindy said it'd be okay."

Simone's mouth fell open. "You mean it? For real?"

Tara nodded and laughed as Simone bounced up and down. Rocky jerked his head back and grunted.

"I'm so glad we're friends," Simone said with a final bounce.

Acceptance filled Tara, creating a warm and fuzzy feeling inside. The feeling turned sour as she turned to see Alissa and Clancy watching her, heads together, evil radiating from Alissa's eyes.

"You okay?" Simone followed her gaze. "Oh, don't let them

get to you, Tara. Alissa is just nasty and you know Clancy...well, he's Clancy."

Tara shivered. "Yeah, but..." She wanted to say...but Alissa is planning something.

Alissa leaned in to Clancy, raised a hand to his ear and whispered, peering back at Tara, a nasty sneer curling her lips. A gold bracelet dangled from her wrist, glimmering in the light from the barn door. Clancy glanced at Tara, shaking his head. Alissa leaned in further and scowled, her mouth moving quickly. Clancy's shoulders sagged as he nodded and headed toward the break room while Alissa spun and strutted out of the barn.

Tara shivered again. Yes, something bad was going to happen. She could feel it.

Simone stroked Rocky's face, chatting about school and how Jon had snuck a fake lizard onto Miss Elizabeth's chair. "You should have seen her. She was so mad!"

"Simone?" Miss Elizabeth called from the end of the aisle. "There you are. Wondered where you'd gone."

"Hi, Miss Elizabeth," Tara called.

"Hi, Tara. How are you?" She smiled broadly and joined the two girls. She looked from Tara to Simone. "I'm so proud of you two girls. You've made such positive improvements at Freedom Farms. Your whole class has, but I think you two have made the most progress."

"Thanks, Miss Elizabeth," Simone said. "I've learned a lot coming here. And I've made good friends, too. Ones my parents will *want* me to hang out with." She grinned at Tara.

Miss Elizabeth glanced down at Simone's tennis shoes. "You need to get your boots on before class."

Simone blushed. "Sorry. I'll get them right now." She looked back at Tara. "Be back in a bit."

Tara nodded and waved as Simone jogged down the aisle toward the break room.

* * * *

Tara watched the others from the top rail of the arena fence. Simone, Philly, and Jon maneuvered their mounts through a small maze of cones, poles, and bridges the volunteers had set up. Miss Elizabeth was right, everyone *had* learned a lot. No one would have been able to get the horses to do this when they first came to Freedom Farms.

Clancy strolled out of the barn, glancing both directions, scuffing his boots back and forth on the ground. Walking to the fence, he peered around the side of the barn. Tara couldn't help but wonder what he was up to. He looked pretty suspicious.

"Simone?" Robin called. "Your turn."

Simone nudged Rocky with her heel, steering him toward three wooden logs on the obstacle course. Rocky stepped over without hesitation. She pulled on the reins, turning him around and wove through the line of cones. Rocky snorted and plodded forward without a glimmer of fear.

"Woo-hoo!" Tara yelled. "Way to go, Simone."

Simone beamed and patted Rocky's shoulder.

"Tara?" Miss Elizabeth called from the gate.

Tara looked over her shoulder. Standing next to Miss Elizabeth was Alissa and Richard. Her heart pounded. Alissa stared back, her mouth twitching in a defiant smirk.

A look of pain lined Miss Elizabeth's face, her eyes darting from Tara to Alissa and back. "I need to see you, Tara."

A shiver of uneasiness whizzed through her. What did they want? Had Alissa set her up once again?

CHAPTER TWENTY

Tara's legs quivered like jelly as she walked to the gate where Miss Elizabeth stood. A nervous shiver caused her hands to tremble and she hid them behind her back. She couldn't let Alissa see she was scared.

Miss Elizabeth cleared her throat. "Tara, Alissa seems to be missing an expensive bracelet. She thinks you might know where it is."

The world swirled around Tara. Her old self would have hidden behind her hair, saying nothing. Before she realized what she was doing, her new self blurted out. "How would I know? I don't know where she keeps her stuff."

"Tara?" Cindy said, walking up behind her. "Is everything okay?"

Tara took a deep breath, trying to decide how to respond. Things weren't okay. Alissa was setting her up again. She just knew it. But she couldn't come out and accuse Alissa of being a liar in front of everyone. That would be suicide.

"Hi, Cindy," Miss Elizabeth interjected. She smiled politely.

"We were just asking Tara a couple of questions. Alissa lost a bracelet. She thinks Tara knows where it is." She looked back to Tara. "Are you sure you haven't seen it?"

Tara shook her head, panic squeezing the air out of her lungs. Mr. McDonald and Sam walked out of the barn and Cindy motioned them over.

Alissa grunted and stared at Miss Elizabeth. "You're not going to let her get away with it, are you?" She stomped her foot and put her hands on her hips. "Tara took it. I know she took it, and I can prove it."

Fear and anger swelled in Tara's throat. "I did not take your-your-whatever it is you said I took." She struggled to keep her voice low, but the emotions quaked through. "I've never taken anything of yours." Her face grew hot despite the shade of the large oak tree.

Mr. McDonald and Sam drew closer to the group.

"Oh, you haven't?" Alissa sneered. "What about my purse? The one you stole in school?"

"You're a liar!" Tara roared. She couldn't help it. She couldn't take it anymore. "I didn't take your stupid purse."

Cindy and Miss Elizabeth stared, their faces filled with surprise at Tara's outburst. Tara slumped back, feeling her old self start to take over again, grabbing her tongue and throwing her into silence.

Alissa snorted. "Then tell them why you're in alternative school." She looked at Richard and Miss Elizabeth. "Tara's a thief. She stole my purse and Principal Jackman found it in her locker. We were nice enough not to press charges." Alissa cocked her head at Tara, one side of her mouth turned up in a wicked smile only she could see. "We didn't press charges then, but I'll make sure Daddy does this time."

Silence surrounded the group. Tara squeezed her fingers into tight fists and hung her head, her old self refusing to let go of her tongue. Her stomach ached as though someone had punched her. She stared from Cindy to Mr. McDonald to Sam, tears welling up in her eyes. She managed a whispered defense. "I didn't do it. Honest. I never took anything of hers." She stared at Cindy. "Please believe me. I'd never steal." Her shoulders slumped and she fell silent again.

She couldn't win. She couldn't prove Alissa was lying. And Alissa was going to destroy everything. They'd kicked her out of school because of Alissa. And now Alissa was going to get her kicked out of Freedom Farms, too.

Richard spoke gruffly, glaring at Tara. "We've had reports of money and other items disappearing from some of our other boarders, too. Maybe we can get to the bottom of all this now."

Tara bit her lip, struggling to keep the tears from flowing. She closed her eyes and waited for the worst, helpless to disprove anything Alissa said.

"Well, I don't believe it," Mr. McDonald snapped and stepped into the circle of people. "If you have proof, Miss Jordan, I want to see it. I won't believe Tara stole anything until then."

Tara searched Mr. McDonald's face. He returned her look, his eyes soft and kind. She glanced to Cindy, whose head nodded in agreement with her father. They believed her? Believed her over Alissa?

"Well, I won't keep my horse where they believe a thief over me," Alissa snorted.

Mr. McDonald straightened his shoulder. "You do whatever you have to do, Miss Jordan."

Tara gawked at Mr. McDonald in silent surprise.

"It is true...about the missing items," Sam interjected. "We've had other boarders complain." He looked at Tara. "But I agree with Mr. McDonald. I don't believe Tara had anything to do with any of it."

Richard looked to Alissa and scowled.

Tara gazed from Cindy to Mr. McDonald to Sam, her eyes brimming with tears. They believed in her.

Cindy stepped up beside Tara, putting an arm around her shoulders, and in a calm, collected voice, she addressed Alissa. "We'd all like to see your proof, Miss Jordan."

Alissa stumbled back, a look of shock contorting her face, her mouth open, gaping like a fish out of water. "You really believe her? You'd believe that trash over me?"

"Miss Jordan," Mr. McDonald growled. "Just because you have been more privileged than Tara, does not mean you have the right to ridicule her." He stepped up on the other side of Tara and put his hand on her shoulder.

Alissa stomped her foot on the ground. "Well, I'll prove to you she stole my bracelet. I took it off in the break room and laid it on the windowsill. I have an eyewitness who saw Tara take it and put it in Trouble's stall."

Cindy and Sam stared at each other.

"Trouble's stall?" Cindy asked.

"That's what I said," Alissa snapped. She threw her blonde ponytail over her shoulder, a smug smile tugging at her mouth.

Tara's jaw twitched. She looked again to Sam, Mr. McDonald, and Cindy. "I didn't take Alissa's bracelet. I didn't!" Her thoughts whirled. She'd seen the bracelet when Alissa was in the hallway with Clancy. So, of course, Clancy was her witness. She'd seen him stomp out of the barn looking only too suspicious.

Had Clancy planted the bracelet in Trouble's stall? Resignation set in. She knew he had. Alissa made sure of it and now, with evidence, everyone would have to believe Alissa. It would be there and Alissa would press charges. She'd lose her friends, the farm, and…Trouble.

A tear trailed down her face. She wanted to run. She wanted

to hide. She glared at Alissa, wanting to rip the evil smile right off her face.

Sam led the small group toward Trouble's stall in the west barn. Tara could feel the eyes of the other students and volunteers following her as they marched across the alleyway between the barns. Shivers slithered up and down her spine as she headed toward certain doom. Alissa strutted behind Sam, her nose tilted upward, Richard lumbering next to her. Mr. McDonald followed them, Tara and Cindy after him, with Miss Elizabeth bringing up the rear. Cindy, her arm still around Tara's shoulder, gave a quick squeeze and a knowing look. Tara looked down at the dirt. She was sure Cindy's look would change when she saw the bracelet. How could it not?

Tara's feet felt heavy as they neared Trouble's stall. Her breath came in short gasps. She looked up as Alissa glanced back, eyes twinkling fiendishly. Terror gripped Tara's throat. Though, this time the panic was not for herself. What would Trouble do at the sight of Alissa. Would he go crazy again? If he hurt someone, Sam would be forced to put him down.

She couldn't let that happen.

"Sam," Tara almost shouted. "Please, Sam, can I get Trouble out of his stall before anyone goes in there?"

"What?" Sam turned to stare at Tara and his eyebrows rose in understanding. "Right, we don't need any trouble."

Alissa snickered and looked at Richard. "Trouble from Trouble? Who would have thought?"

Richard grinned, but only for a moment. His eyes darted from Alissa to Mr. McDonald to Sam.

Sam frowned and continued, "That's a good idea, Tara. Go ahead and get him out."

Alissa turned on Sam. "What? You're going to let *her* go in and get rid of the evidence?"

Sam's jaw twitched. "Miss Jordan…Miss Elizabeth, Mr.

McDonald and I will be right here with Tara. Don't you think it is a wise idea to get the horse out of the stall so we can search the area thoroughly?"

For a change, all eyes were on Alissa. She stood speechless, her face reddening, before nodding in agreement.

Tara hurried past Alissa and continued down the aisle with Sam and Mr. McDonald on either side. She looked at Sam out of the corner of her eye. She wanted to tell him she'd been set up...wanted to tell him how much she appreciated his support and she'd never steal...never! But her old self kept her tongue in check. She grabbed Trouble's lead from the nail outside the stall and reached for the door.

"Here, Trouble," she cooed, stepping through the half door, held open by Mr. McDonald. She snapped the lead to Trouble's halter and led him out of the stall, away from Alissa. At least she'd saved *him* from Alissa's wrath.

The minutes dragged as the men scoured Trouble's stall. Tara leaned her cheek into Trouble's velvety soft muzzle. "Any minute now," she whispered to him. "My world is going to change. I can't get out of this one. Alissa set me up again and there's no way out."

Trouble blew a long warm breath onto Tara's face and whickered low, the sound rumbling in his long neck.

Tara looked into Trouble's eyes, contemplating her options. Maybe she should go along with it. Tell them she took it and say she was sorry. Maybe they'd let her stay. Maybe...

Tara winced as she thought of the school principal's last words before he sent her to alternative school—next time juvie hall.

There was no "maybe" to anything. Alissa would never let her stay at the farm.

She hugged Trouble's neck, a sob vibrating in her chest. "I'm going to miss you so much," she whispered.

Mr. McDonald stepped out of the stall and faced Miss Elizabeth. "I can't find anything. Richard, Sam? You find anything?"

Richard stepped out of the stall, shaking his head.

Sam followed. "Not a thing."

Tara's heart somersaulted with surprised confusion. Nothing? Were they saying that to protect her? No. Not Richard.

"What?" Alissa screeched, pushing Miss Elizabeth to the side. "Obviously, you missed it. It's got to be there. Clanc...er, I mean, my witness said he saw her put it right there." She stormed to the stall entrance and searched the wooden walls, kicking straw and overturning the feed bucket. "It's got to be here."

Cindy smiled at Tara. "Well, Alissa, it appears your eyewitness was wrong."

Alissa rumbled and stomped out of the stall.

"Miss E." Clancy jogged down the aisle to the group. "Hey, Miss E." He waved and pointed toward Alissa. "I found it. I found Alissa's bracelet."

Tara looked at Clancy, totally confused.

"What?" Alissa sputtered as she ran up and grabbed at the swinging bracelet held gingerly between Clancy's fingers. Her mouth twisted as she flung the piece of jewelry on the dirt floor. Chunks of brown and green goo stuck to the dangles and an offensive odor sifted through the hall. Alissa stooped to pick it up, holding it away from her by the clasp, turning her face as she gagged. "What's all over it?"

"Oh, sorry 'bout that," Clancy grinned. "I found it in a pile of horse crap. It must have fallen there."

Alissa's face reddened. "What? You were...a..." She turned to Richard. "Tara must have thrown it there. She stole it, I tell you. She took it from the break room."

Clancy shook his head. "No, I don't think so. I saw you wearing it when you came out of the break room. It must have fallen off."

Alissa stuttered. "I…uh…it…" She let out a long growl, "Ohh!" and stomped down the aisle.

Tara faked a cough as she tried to cover up her laughter. She'd never seen Alissa so mad before. Her new self rose up again, basking in the joy of friends who believed in and supported her.

CHAPTER TWENTY-ONE

Tara glanced at the clock through the doorway on the porch. Eleven o'clock. She turned to watch the road again.

Where was she? How long did it take for her to drive out here?

She twiddled the pen in her hand and stuffed it back into the spiral binding of her journal, too anxious to write. Simone was coming.

The last two weeks had flown by. The final class at Freedom Farms ended in a blur as Tara tried to put Alissa's accusation behind her and say her teary goodbyes to her classmates. Even Clancy grinned and waved as Miss Elizabeth's van disappeared down the driveway for the final time.

Tara couldn't help but wonder what happened that day. She hadn't talked to any of the class since, except for the brief phone call with Simone to set up the sleepover. Had Alissa's plan backfired? Did Clancy really find the bracelet in horse poop? She smiled. It didn't matter now. What mattered most was Cindy, Sam, and Mr. McDonald had believed her. They believed her over Alissa.

Mr. Jordan had moved their horses to another farm the next day, surely at the badgering of his daughter. Mr. McDonald didn't seem the least bit upset about losing their business. And Tara wasn't sad to see Alissa leave either.

Tara lifted her head up as a car zoomed down the highway. It kept on driving, past the farm. She put the journal on the small table between the two Adirondack chairs and leaned over, tracing a board with the toe of her boot.

With therapy classes over, Tara had focused on the final assignments Miss Elizabeth had given her. She finished the school year with the best grades she'd ever gotten—three A's and two B's. Tara was free to return to high school in the fall. But what high school? Tara still didn't know.

Cindy had waited nervously to hear if Scarborough Farms had any training positions open. She'd received the phone call yesterday, thrilled with the job offer of assistant trainer position starting in September. It was bittersweet news for Tara. She was happy for Cindy. She also knew it meant she would have to return to foster care…again.

Well, she'd known it was only temporary.

Tara sighed and shook her head. She didn't want to think of anything sad today. Simone, her friend, was coming to stay the weekend. Her hands trembled with excitement as she waited for her very first sleepover.

A car honked and pulled into the driveway. Tara jumped up. "Hey, Simone."

Cindy opened the front door and peeked out. "I take it your friend is here?"

Tara laughed and hopped off the porch, meeting the car as it parked on the gravel drive in front of Cindy's house. After dropping Simone's bags in Tara's room, the girls left Cindy visiting with Simone's mother in the kitchen and dashed to the barn. Trouble hung his head over the stall door and whickered as Tara entered the barn.

"Oh, Tara, he's so pretty." Simone reached to pet Trouble's blazed face, stopping in mid-reach and looked at Tara. "Is he going to bite me?"

"No, he's a big pussy cat." She smiled and rubbed his nose. "He trusts me and doesn't act crazy anymore at all."

Simone stroked his face. "I don't know how you did it, but I'm glad you did. I bet Alissa was livid when she found out." Simone's mouth dropped open. "Oh my gosh, speaking of Alissa, I forgot to tell you."

Trouble startled and Tara laid a reassuring hand on his cheek. "Tell me what?"

"Alissa and Clancy are through. It was all over right after our last session here at the farm."

"They are?" A small smirk lifted one side of Tara's mouth. It was so evil for her to be happy, but she couldn't help it. "Did it have anything to do with what happened at the last horse therapy class?"

Simone nodded, grinning.

"So what did happen? I was sure Clancy had planted Alissa's bracelet in Trouble's stall so I'd get blamed."

"It's so funny," Simone snickered, her eyes dancing with amusement. "Apparently, Clancy has a crush on you."

"What?" Tara stared in disbelief. All Clancy ever wanted to do was make her life miserable. Get even with her for what she'd done her first day. "How do you know all this anyway?"

Simone laughed. "Clancy told Jon. And you know Jon…he can't keep a secret." She wiped a happy tear from the corner of her eye. "Clancy even told Jon you 'looked pretty fine' with your hair pulled back."

Tara shook her head. "I can't even come close to being as pretty as Alissa. And she so popular. And rich…"

Simone snorted. "Well, she may be pretty on the outside, but her rotten, evil self spoils her good looks once you get to know her. Guess Clancy finally saw that."

Tara ginned, silently agreeing.

Simone prattled on. "Anyway, he was going to tell Alissa to kiss off that day we saw them in the barn. She's so bossy, you know. Before he could, they saw us. Remember?"

Tara nodded.

"Well, before he could say anything, she laid out her plan with the bracelet. He didn't want to do it. She got real mad. Said if he didn't do it, she'd tell her daddy *he* stole the bracelet and *he'd* be the one in trouble."

"No way."

Simone nodded. "Yes, way. Clancy said he had no choice but go along with her. He took the bracelet, but didn't hide it in the stall. Instead he dropped it in a pile of horse crap behind the barn and ground it in with his boot, making it nice and gooey."

"That's so gross." Tara could only imagine how slimy the bracelet had been when Clancy handed it to Alissa. No wonder she dropped it so fast.

Simone giggled. "Clancy thinks you're pretty cool now. What did you say to him?"

"What do you mean?"

"He told Jon you'd said something to him...something nice. Surprised him. I didn't realize you ever talked to him."

Tara knew what Simone was talking about. "I didn't really talk to him." She scratched Trouble's ear, giving him a chunk of carrot. "I just felt sorry for him that day he got dumped in the water. It could have been any one of us and I told him so."

The weekend passed quickly. Tara showed Simone the farm, riding the trails through the trees at the back of the barns. They shared stories and laughs, chatting about horses, school, and boys. She'd never had a friend to confide in before, even though there were still some things she guarded close to her heart.

After supper on Sunday, Tara and Simone joined Cindy and Sam on the porch. Tara sat on the plank steps watching the sun set and enjoying the cool evening air.

"What are you grinning about?" Sam interrupted her bliss.

"What?" Tara jumped and looked up at Sam. She couldn't see his eyes, the glow from the yard-light casting dark shadows under his ball cap. His mouth curved up in a semi-smile.

"You look like you've won the lottery or something," Sam continued.

"Hmmm," Tara murmured, leaning back against the porch rail. The tiny lights of a million fireflies blinked on and off in the growing darkness, like a jumbled strand of Christmas lights. "I was just thinking. You don't see fireflies in the city. And the stars seem so much brighter out here, too." She stared up into the heavens, gazing from star to star.

"They do, don't they?" Simone said, following her gaze. "I never realized there were so many."

Sam grunted, contented. "And what about the quiet? There's no such thing as quiet in the city, is there

Tara shook her head, her loose hair   g over her shoulders. She adjusted the headband that kept it neatly away from her face. "Yeah. I really don't want to go back there."

Cindy put down her papers. "What do you mean, Tara?"

Tara held her breath realizing what she had said. She looked out at the barn, her lower lip quivering. Suddenly her happy, peaceful world seemed to fade away.

She *didn't* want to go back to the city. Didn't want to go back to foster care. Tears welled up in her eyes.

Sam leaned forward in his chair. "What are you saying, Tara?"

Tara shook her head, looking away. She swiped at her eyes, hoping no one could see her face. "Nothing." She stared at the

barn, her heart aching.

"Tara?" Sam began again, his voice low and soft. "We can't help if we don't know what's wrong."

Tara looked up at Sam, his eyes now revealed in the light. Her throat tightened.

Where should she start?

"Oh my gosh," Cindy gasped, crinkling the papers, a pained expression crossing her face. "You're wondering what's going to happen to you when I go to Scarborough Farms, aren't you?"

Simone gasped with understanding and put a supportive hand on Tara's shoulder.

Tara looked down at her lap, picking at the hem of her T-shirt. "I've never felt I belonged anywhere...until now." Her voice cracked. "I have friends here. I like it here. I don't want to leave. And how can I say good-bye to Trouble? I love him so much." She wasn't sure when they'd started, but tears spilled down her face.

Simone squeezed her shoulder. "I'll always be your friend. No matter what. And maybe you can stay on with Cindy's parents. Or Sam."

Tara shook her head. "No. Cindy's dad has to take care of her mom and the farm. He's going to be really busy when Cindy leaves."

Sam frowned. "And I doubt they'd let me be a foster, not with a young lady."

Tara pulled her knees up and wrapped her arms around them. "Well, I knew it was only temporary when I came. I just didn't think it was going to be so hard to say good-bye."

"I'm so sorry," Cindy said, lifting a hand to her forehead, like she was searching for an answer in the middle of her thoughts. "Maybe I can ask Scarborough Farms to wait..."

"No!" Tara almost yelled, spinning to face Cindy. "You have to go. This was your dream. I'd feel even worse if I knew you didn't go because of me." She meant it. If Cindy stayed, she'd feel guilty every day, seeing her and knowing what she'd given up. Finally, she spoke again, her words slow and low. "I've learned so much since I came here. I've learned a lot about horses. And I've learned a lot about me, too. I won't like going back to foster care, but I'll be okay. I'll manage. I'm stronger than I thought. I'm really going to miss Trouble, though." She looked up at Sam. "You'll take good care of him, won't you?"

Sam nodded, his eyes moist. He spoke softly. "Tara, you are more mature than a lot of adults I know." He gave her a sad smile. "You know you will always be a part of us, no matter where you go. We're all friends here. Family. That will never change. And as far as Trouble is concerned...no matter where you are, I'll make sure you get back here to help me with him. He needs you as much as you need him."

Tara swiped at her eyes and searched Sam's face. "You really mean it?"

"You bet I do," he said. "After what you've done for him, it's the least I can do."

Cindy stood up, wiping her streaked face. "I need a tissue..." she said, opening the screen door. "...before I blubber all over these papers and smear all the ink. I'll get us all something to drink, too, okay?"

Simone hopped up, swiping at her face as well. "I'll help you."

The door clicked shut behind them. Tara wiped her cheek on her sleeve. "You really mean it, Sam? You'll let me come out to see Trouble?"

Sam looked Tara in the eye. "I'd never lie to you."

The words touched Tara's heart. No one had ever cared enough to say that to her, let alone mean it. She smiled and gazed at the barn, wondering what Trouble was doing, wondering if he had any inkling of how their lives might change in seven short

weeks. Glasses chinked inside the house, followed by the suction sound of the refrigerator closing.

She turned to Sam again. "How come you don't have any kids? You'd make a great dad."

Sam sat silent. He leaned back in his chair, the shadows returning to hide his eyes. He cleared his throat and said, "I wanted a family. I was even going to get married once. Loved a gal a lot. Except, she didn't love me back. She up and left one day. Tore my whole world apart."

"I'm sorry, Sam." Tara stared at the wooden floor. "My mom did, too. It stinks. Guess we both know how it feels."

Sam grunted and rocked back and forth. "I guess we do." He drummed his fingers on the chair and gazed out to the barns. "You know, the county horse show is coming up next month. Do you want to try your hand at running Trouble in the barrel race?"

Tara looked at him, her melancholy giving way to excitement. "Do you think we could be ready?" Her insides tickled like the buzzing of a bumblebee hive.

CHAPTER TWENTY-TWO

Trouble pranced in the end of the arena, his muscles tense, ears erect. Tara chewed the edge of her lip and eyed the barrels in the arena, running the cloverleaf pattern in her head the way Sam had taught her. She turned Trouble toward the first barrel and urged him forward.

"Now, Trouble," she pressed. "Go!"

Trouble took off, galloping toward the first drum, ears laid flat against his head. Tara bent forward, her head and body low. Laying the reins against his red neck, she braced for the first turn of the pattern. Trouble leaned and raced around the barrel, missing it by inches. Tara straightened their course and headed him toward the second barrel. Wind whipped at her ponytail, mingling her brown strands with Trouble's black mane. She laid the reins against the opposite side of his neck, ready for the next rotation. In a flying change of leads, Trouble tilted toward the drum, whipped around and sprinted toward the third and final barrel.

"You can do it, Trouble," Tara whispered into his flattened

ears. Tears streamed from her eyes as the wind whistled past her. Once more, she laid the reins against his neck and he circled the drum so close she felt the rounded rim brush against her knee. Tara straightened him out for the final run home, gripping his sides tightly with her thighs, pressing him faster.

"Come on, Trouble. Go, go, *go!*"

Trouble sped down the middle of the arena like a rocket, his long tail jetting behind, a blaze of black fire.

"Whoo hoo," Sam hooted. "Your best time ever."

Beaming, Tara pulled Trouble to a trot and circled him around the end of the arena, patting his neck. He grunted, blowing out a long breath.

"If only Alissa would have raced him," Tara panted. "Rather than trying to force him to be something he wasn't, she'd…"

"She'd be the one racing him instead of you?"

Tara jumped and hunted for the person who had finished her sentence. Janie leaned against the fence on the opposite side of the arena.

She smiled and waved. "Sorry, didn't mean to scare you or anything. Happened to be passing by and stopped to watch. Great run. You're going to give Red and me a run for the money."

Tara felt her cheeks grow warm. "Thanks." She patted Trouble's shoulder. "I can't take the credit, though. It's all Trouble."

Janie walked around the ring toward Sam. "Yeah, he *is* fast. I don't think Alissa could have ever gotten him to run like that, though. It's because of you, Tara. Trouble will do almost anything for *you*. Everyone can see it."

Sam agreed. "You know she's right, Tara. We all see it."

A smile spread across her face.

"I can't believe he's the same horse." Janie continued, talking to Sam. "I didn't think it was possible to turn him around. He hated Alissa. She was so sure he was going to kill someone. You guys sure proved her wrong."

Tara dismounted and pulled a chuck of carrot from her pocket to offer Trouble, listening to them talk. There was something in Janie's voice. She'd heard it somewhere before. Tara turned to stare at Janie, remembering where. She'd been the one talking to Alissa that day outside Trouble's stall. She was Alissa's friend.

"Are you racing in the big show next week?" Janie asked, looking from Tara to Sam. "He looks ready."

Sam looked toward Tara. "Have to ask her. She's my rider. Are we going to run?"

Tara eyed Janie, her old self throwing up her guard. Was she up to something? Setting up another trap from Alissa?

Trouble rubbed his ear on Tara's shoulder and pushed her forward, crunching his carrot and nodding his head up and down.

Janie laughed. "Well, I guess Trouble says you are."

Tara grinned. Uncertainty still nagged at her, but it was hard not to like Janie. She was kind and friendly. Nothing like Alissa.

"Well." Janie wiped her hands on her jeans. "Are you all done practicing for today?"

Sam nodded. "Yeah, you can have the arena if you like."

"Great," Janie said. "I need to practice Red. Especially now, since we've got such stiff competition." She winked and headed toward the barn entrance.

Tara watched after her, stroking Trouble's neck and leading him toward the gate. Something moved at the side of the barn, a shadow blurring across the white boards. Tara raised a hand to shield her eyes from the glare. Whatever it was, was gone.

"You coming?" Sam asked as he walked toward the barn after Janie.

"I think I'll stay out here for a while if you don't mind," she said, loosening Trouble's cinch. "I want to watch Janie practice."

"Sure. She can give you some good tips," he called.

Tara stripped the saddle from Trouble's back and set it on the wooden hitching rail next to the arena. Would Janie give her racing tips? She seemed nice enough. Still…she was Alissa's friend.

The scent of roses tickled Tara's nose and she turned to rose garden on the hill, a sadness tugging at her as she thought of Jupiter and Cindy. The garden seemed to sparkle in the morning sun. It *was* a beautiful tribute. Mrs. McDonald waved from her rocking chair on the porch. Tara waved back, glad she was okay and back home now. She tied Trouble's rein to the bar next to the saddle and jogged up the hill.

"Hi Mrs. McDonald," she panted. "It's good to see you outside. How are you feeling?"

Mrs. McDonald smiled and patted Tara's hand. "I'm just fine, honey. Thanks for asking." She peeked at the door and leaned in to whisper to Tara. "You know, I've been home for over a week now and this is the first time Mr. McDonald has let me out of his sight. He's worse than an old mother hen."

Tara laughed. "Well, he cares about you. We all do. We're glad to have you home."

Mrs. McDonald leaned back and smiled, her whole face lighting up. "I am too. Even if my husband is a little overprotective." She pointed to a plate of slightly burnt brownies. "Want a brownie? They're a little overdone. But he's trying." She winked.

Tara grinned and reached for the plate.

A series of loud *BANGS,* like firecrackers, blasted from the barn. Tara spun around as a horse screamed inside, followed by a girl shouting. Her eyes darted to Trouble. Still tied to the bar, he watched the barn door, head erect, body tense.

Tara dropped the brownie and raced toward him. The horse

inside the barn screamed again, followed by a *CRASH* and the sound of splintering wood. Smoke belched out the window. The girl inside shrieked.

Tara slowed up as she reached Trouble. She had to get him out of there. Laying a reassuring hand on his withers, she could feel his body tremble as he stared at the smoking barn. A flash of chestnut whizzed out the door and Red raced into the open, reins dangling wildly around his legs, stirrups flapping as he bucked. A second blur ran down the aisle inside the door and Tara recognized Sam dashing in the direction Red had come. Knowing Trouble was safe, she darted toward the running horse, snagging Red's reins before he could get away.

Red jerked against the reins, his eyes wild with fright, twisting and turning as people came dashing from all directions, shouting and grabbing buckets. Tara recognized some of them. Some had horses boarded at the farm. Others took lessons. But all were here with one thing on their mind, to put out whatever was causing the smoke in the barn.

Tara coaxed Red to her and led him to the hitching post, his feet dancing with each step as he stared back at the barn. She forced herself to stay calm, running her hand down Red's neck and inspecting him for injuries.

Mr. McDonald appeared beside her. "Are you okay, Tara? What happened?"

"We're okay." She swallowed. "I don't know what happened. I heard a loud bang, saw smoke, and then Red came running out."

A figure staggered out of the barn. "Call an ambulance," Sam yelled. Janie lay limp in his arms, like a rag doll. Her leg twisted in an awkward position and a large red gash oozed blood from her forehead.

A tall man dropped his bucket and pulled out his cellphone, tapping at the numbers. Tara half-heard him talking to the operator, unable to grasp his words. All she could focus on was Janie's unconscious form. Sam laid her on the ground while Mr. McDonald ran to the water pump next to the barn and whipped out his handkerchief. He rushed back to Sam with the moistened cloth, hovering behind them as Sam wiped Janie's face. Her eyelids fluttered and opened.

"What? What's going on? Where's Red?" She moved to raise her head and fell back to the ground, a low cry of pain rolling from her mouth.

Tara stroked Red's neck, feeling a new respect for this Janie. Despite her injuries, her first thoughts were for her horse.

"Tara's got Red," Sam said quietly. "She'll take good care of him. Don't move. We've called an ambulance."

Sam continued to speak soft and low. Tara couldn't hear his words. All she heard was Janie's painful moaning. Red heard it, too. He pranced and danced around her, eyes rimmed in white, jerking to look at Janie, lying on the ground.

Trouble whickered. He stood alert but calm, watching Tara. She led Red to where he was tied, and directed them both across the driveway, away from the confusion surrounding the accident.

The ambulance arrived, as well as a second car which, from the sounds of the concerned voices, carried Janie's parents. Long minutes passed. EMT's rushed and loaded Janie's gurney. People passed buckets of water. Janie's mother cried. Finally the ambulance crunched back down the gravel driveway and revved up the highway, siren blaring, with Janie's parents right behind it.

Sam joined Tara across the driveway. "You okay?"

Trouble and Red grazed, raising their heads to watch the chaos at the barn every so often. Tara patted Red's shoulder. "Is Janie going to be okay?"

"She's got a broken leg. Maybe a concussion, too. The doctors will take care of her."

The confusion was dying down. The bucket brigade had

disbanded and people stood around in small groups, talking, as Mr. McDonald surveyed the damage.

"What happened, Sam?"

Tara could see he was upset. He grit his teeth, his voice rumbling. "It looks like someone tossed a bunch of firecrackers in one of the stalls." He glanced at Trouble. "Into Trouble's stall."

Tara gasped. Horror filled her as she thought out loud. "What if he'd been in there?"

Sam shook his head. "I'm just glad you decided to stay outside. Otherwise, he would have been."

Tara struggled to breathe, feeling as if someone had thrown her into a vacuum and sucked all the air out of her lungs. If she hadn't stayed to watch Janie, Trouble *would* have been in his stall. He could have been...killed.

Instinctively she moved closer to Trouble, feeling the warmth of his shoulder. "Do you think someone was trying to hurt him?"

Sam's mouth formed a straight line. "I don't know. Did someone deliberately do it? Or was it some stupid Fourth of July prank? With the holiday next week, I've been kind of worried. Sometimes kids do stupid things. But if I find the person who did this...I'll..."

He heaved an angry sigh and continued, "Richard's cleaning up the mess in there. It started some of the straw on fire and charred the wood. But we got it put out before it did any structural damage. I'll put Red back in his stall. His is okay since he's housed at the other end of the barn. I'll have to find a new one for Trouble. We're lucky most of the horses in that barn are out to pasture right now or it could have been a lot worse than it was."

Sam led Red back to the barn, leaving Tara to her thoughts. She leaned against Trouble's shoulder, biting her lip, imagining what Trouble's stall must look like. What if he'd been in there? Was someone out to hurt him? To stop them from competing in the barrel race next week?

CHAPTER TWENTY-THREE

Trucks and horse-trailers filled the dirt parking lot. Big ones, small ones. Expensive ones, not-so-expensive ones. Horses of all colors and sizes stood by the trailers or were being ridden or led from place to place. English saddles here, Western gear there. People swarmed the fairgrounds like bees in a working beehive, the buzz growing louder and louder.

Tara turned in a circle, watching the activity, amazed at the organized chaos, excited to be a part of it.

A young girl walked back from the large arena, leading a pretty Pinto colt from halter class, beaming as she waved a purple rosette ribbon in her hand. Tara couldn't help feel an ache of jealousy as the girl's mother and father surrounded her, hugging her, showering her with accolades and praise.

With a sigh, she turned and opened the small metal door at the front of Freedom Farm's long horse trailer and pulled out the feed net. From the back of the pick-up, she selected a small section of hay. Trouble snorted and raised his head, nickering to the other horses. A large gray, two trailers away, returned his call with a whinny of his own.

Trouble was excited, too, Tara could tell. Stamping his feet, ears perked so far forward she thought they were going to touch together like a set of jumper cables and send electric sparks all over the fairground. She slid a hand down his shoulder, checking his lead and making sure the knot was secure. "Did you find yourself a new friend?" she asked, rubbing his ears.

Sam carried two buckets around the side of the trailer, one of water and the other filled with brushes and picks. His arms showed a nervous tension, mechanically moving to take care of the business at hand. But his face radiated with pleasure. He tossed Tara a brush. "You nervous?"

She knew he could tell by the look on her face. There was no hiding it. "My stomach is flip-flopping so much I feel like I'm going to be sick."

He dumped the rest of brushes on the ground and held the empty bucket up to her face, eyes teasing. "Well, get it out now, rather than in the ring."

Tara forced a small smile at his mock sympathy. His combination of seriousness and humor was the medicine she needed. She took the bucket, shaking her head. "No, I don't think I'll need it, but I never realized there'd be so many people here."

Sam gazed around the fairgrounds, trading nods with a tall man with a big, black mare. "Hey, Tom. Porsche is looking really good this year."

He seemed to know almost everyone. Positioning the bucket of water for Trouble he turned his attention back to Tara. "It's a big show. There's actually people here from all over the state. Two rings going with so many. Halter and Pleasure classes are this morning. Barrels aren't until this afternoon. So you've got plenty of time to get calmed down."

Tara blinked, butterflies fluttering inside again at the

mention of barrels. "Or get more nervous."

A couple of teens walked toward a ritzy black horse trailer, their heads bent close together, talking in muffled voices, dirty looks aimed at Tara and Trouble.

"That's the one," one girl said. "Alissa told me about him. Stay clear of him or he'll tear your head off, she said."

The second girl stared, eyes filled with fear. "How can they allow him to be here? And that girl? Alissa said she belongs in jail."

Tara lowered her head. Because of Alissa, Trouble's reputation haunted him as much as hers did.

Seeing her look, Sam reassured her. "Don't worry, Tara. Stupid people say stupid things."

She gave him a small smile. "I'm trying. We'll show them all today. Show them what kind of horse Trouble really is."

An attention-getting cough sounded behind them and Tara turned around to see Janie, leaning on her crutches, a pink cast covering three quarters of her leg, disappearing under a pair of loose-fitting shorts. A tall slender woman with the same hair and eyes stood next to her.

"I didn't think I'd see you here today," Tara said. "How are you?"

Janie smiled at her mother. "I begged Mom to at least let me come watch, even if I can't ride. I had to root you guys on."

Her mother smiled, her pride for her daughter showing in her face. "She didn't just beg. She threatened to drive herself here if I didn't bring her." She offered her hand to Sam. "I'm Georgia."

Sam shook Georgia's hand. "We're glad to see her up and around," Sam said. "Is the leg okay?"

Janie nodded. "The cast sucks. But the doctor says it should heal fine." She looked up at Tara, emotions welling in her eyes. "I had to stop by and say thanks for taking care of Red last week.

I would have died if anything would have happened to him."

Tara smiled. "Of course. I'd feel the same way. He's a nice horse and I was glad I was there to help."

Janie frowned, biting back the tears welling up. "He's really gentle. But that firecracker…scared him. He reared up and I lost his reins. It was stupid—I ran in front of him, trying to catch him. He didn't see me what with the smoke and all. Such a stupid thing to do."

"I'm just glad Red didn't get hurt and you're going to be okay," Tara replied. "They're still trying to find out who threw it."

"Well, I hope they find them," Janie growled. She took a breath, her face turning serious. "I wanted to come over and warn you…keep a close eye on Trouble, okay?" She glanced over at her mother and back to Tara. "Alissa's been on a rampage since she found out you were racing Trouble in barrels. She called me the other day. Said she'd heard about my accident and had the nerve to ask me, since I couldn't ride Red today, if she could race him. When I told her no, she went berserk."

Janie seemed lost in her own thoughts as she rambled on, her voice both angry and worried. "There's no way I'm letting her ride Red. She's made Solomon a nervous wreck in just a few short weeks. No way is she touching Red."

She closed her eyes and swallowed, seemingly aware how angry her voice was sounding. She looked at Sam, searching his face for an answer. "Until Tara came, all Alissa could ever talk about was riding Dressage. Now, today, Mr. Jordan told me she's riding Solomon in barrels. Solomon's *never* run barrels!"

Janie turned back to Tara. "Everyone always thought Trouble was the problem, thought he was wild and mean. I seriously think the problem is Alissa."

Tara didn't know what to say. She'd known it. Now others were finally seeing it. It should make her happy, right? So why wasn't she?

Janie leaned in, taking hold of Tara's forearm, staring into her eyes. "Alissa's going to try and rattle you. That's what she does. Don't let her do it." She released her grip. "Stay calm and let Trouble run. He's got the heart to win this thing for you."

Tara stood silent, unable to speak. She could feel the fear sneak up her spine, snake-like, ready to strike.

"It'll be fine, Tara." She felt Sam's callused hand on her shoulder. "We appreciate the warning, Janie. At least now we know to be on the look-out."

Tara nodded. Though her eyes stared at Janie, she couldn't see her. Dark clouds invaded her thoughts, a clammy cold spreading up her arms and shoulders, strangling her. Alissa's voice warbled in her head, "She'll be sorry. I'll make sure of it."

"Thanks again, Janie," Sam called, jolting Tara from her nightmare. Janie hobbled away toward the stands, her mother close beside her. The announcer's voice boomed across the lot, announcing the next class.

Tara jumped as Trouble blew out a loud breath. Trouble. What if Alissa tried to hurt him? What if she couldn't protect him?

"Are you okay?" Sam asked, turning Tara to face him, searching her eyes.

Tara couldn't hide the fear in her eyes.

Sam took Tara's hands in his own and said, "Alissa is all talk. She won't try and do anything to Trouble. Not here. We won't let her." His voice was soothing, calm. "I think you know you've got a lot of people here who love and support you. And you've got a horse willing to do anything you ask."

She smiled, the worry slithering back into the recesses of her mind. "You're right. And Trouble is going to show everyone once and for all he's not the beast Alissa portrayed him to be. We'll show them."

Sam grinned and put his hands on his hips. "That's my girl. I'm going to go get your number. Will you be okay for a little while?"

Tara nodded, resting a hand on Trouble's shoulder. "We'll be fine." As Sam headed to the judge's booth, she wrapped her arms around Trouble's neck and hugged him, a boost of confidence warming her. "We're more than fine, aren't we Trouble? We have each other. We can take anything Alissa throws at us, can't we? We'll show her. And even if I can't be there every day after Cindy leaves, Sam promised we'll still see each other."

She busied herself, brushing Trouble's coat to a deep crimson glow. She pulled her saddle from the back of Sam's pick-up and sat down, rubbing saddle soap into the brown leather, cleaning it to a rich luster.

"Tara?" a woman's voice called from the front of the pick-up.

Tara looked up. Her eyes widened, wondering if she was seeing a ghost. "Mom? Is that you?" She jumped to her feet, her heart beating faster and faster, her hands trembling. "What are you doing here?"

Her mother's mouth curved up on one side, brows furrowed deep into her forehead. "Well, is that how you greet your momma after all this time?"

Tara couldn't breathe. Her mother was here? Was this a dream? Nervous shivers zapped her as her mother strolled closer, stopping directly in front of her. She reached out and clumsily wrapped her in an awkward hug. Tara stiffened, and with a deep sigh, closed her eyes, letting her body go limp in the bony arms surrounding her. She had dreamed of this, yearned for it for so long. Tears filled her eyes and a sob swelled in her throat. "Oh, Mom!"

Her mother pushed her back, staring into her face with hard

eyes. "Are you crying?" she asked gruffly.

Tara swiped at her eyes, trying to swallow her embarrassment. "I'm sorry. I guess…I'm so happy to see you."

Her mother tried to smile, her gaunt cheeks twitching. "Well, I'm happy to see you, too." Her voice was all sweet and syrupy. She looked Tara up and down. "You've really grown since I saw you last."

Tara sniffed and rubbed at her nose. Since she'd seen her last? Five years ago. "How did you find me?"

Tara's mother gazed around at the crowds of people mingling everywhere. She seemed uncomfortable, searching for the right words. "Does it matter? I'm here now. I wanted to see you. I want you…I want you to come back with me."

Shock flashed across Tara's face. "Come back? Back where?"

Her mother let out an exasperated sigh. "Home. I want you to come home with me. Where else?" She looked around and nervously opened and closed her purse.

"Home? You want me to go home?" Tara's heart raced. This is what she had dreamed of for years. To go home with her mother. To be a family. So, why did it feel so wrong?

Sam had said they were almost family. Cindy loved her. Sam. Trouble.

She frowned. "Where's home?"

"Home…with me. I'll show you." Her mother motioned for Tara to follow as she marched toward the front of the pick-up.

Tara stood still, frozen in thought. She looked back at Trouble's trusting eyes and shook her head. Would home be someplace close? So she could remain near Trouble? Would her mother be proud of her, watching her race today?

"Come on, Tara" her mother demanded. "I haven't got all day."

Tara jerked out of her stupor. "What do you mean? I can't leave now." She pointed to Trouble, munching hay beside the trailer. "I can't leave Trouble. We have a race this afternoon." She moved close to Trouble, wrapping one arm around his neck. "Don't you want to hear about him? He's my best friend." She couldn't stop her tongue, the questions eating at her. "And...and don't you want to know what I've been doing all these years?"

Her mother's eyes darted quickly. "Of course I want to hear. Later. Right now, we have to go. I have to meet someone."

"Meet someone?" Tara held her ground, her new self poised and assertive. What was her mother up to? "Who? Why?"

Tara's mother stared her in the eye. "How dare you be sassy with me," she said icily. She paused and opened her purse, pulling out a cigarette. "I mean..." Her voice turned sickly sweet. "...we can talk after my meeting. I know we have a lot to catch up on."

Tara returned her mother's stare. "A lot to catch up on?" That was an understatement. "You've been gone over five years."

Her mother rolled her eyes, pulling out a lighter to light her cigarette. Thee muscles in her cheek tightened, clearly struggling not to show her anger. "I know, I know. But I want you to come with me now." She reached a skinny hand toward Tara, motioning her to follow. Cigarette smoke circled around her mother's head like an eerie halo.

Tara shook her head, holding onto Trouble a little tighter. "I told you I can't leave Trouble. We're racing this afternoon. Don't you want to watch?"

Her mother snorted. "You mean you are actually riding those filthy creatures?" She eyed Trouble with disgust and took a drag of her cigarette. "You must take after your father."

Tara jolted at the reference. "My father? My father liked horses? You never told me that. You said he was a rodeo clown."

Her mother stared back at her, obviously shaken with her slip-up. "Well...it doesn't matter. He chose horses and rodeos over you, didn't he?"

Tara flinched and stared at the ground, fighting back a tear. Trouble turned his head and sniffed at her free hand, his breath soft and warm. "I have to stay here, Mom. I owe it to Trouble to win this race."

Her mother cackled. "Win?" she scoffed, taking one more step closer, seeming to notice the lapse in Tara's confidence at the mention of her father. "What have you ever won in your life? You need to put this foolish notion out of your head and come with me...*now!*"

Tara jumped at the abruptness. The sweetness was gone from her mother's voice, replaced with the anger she'd always known. "No. I'm not going anywhere with you. You up and leave me...disappear from my life and then expect me to drop everything important to me and go with you? I can't."

Her mother grabbed Tara's arm, fingernails digging into her flesh. "You will do what I tell you to, young lady. I'm still your mother."

Tara pulled back. Her mother hung on. Trouble raised his head, his eyes flashing. He stomped at the ground and screamed a loud warning.

Tara's mother slipped backward, her face paling with terror. "You keep that beast away from me. She told me about him. He's crazy."

Tara reached up and grabbed Trouble's halter, stroking his muzzle to calm him down. She surveyed her mother, dreading the next question. "Who told you about Trouble?"

"Well...I...ahh," her mother stepped backward, gawking around at the people stopped to watch them. "Does it matter who I heard it from? I just know they call him Trouble."

Tara's breath came in short bursts, the suspicion overwhelming her senses. She pressed on. "How did you find me? Who told you I was here? And why now?"

Her mother took another step backward. "I…ah…" She looked around, rubbing her shaky hands together, the ashes from the cigarettes flipping to the ground.

"Who told you he was called Trouble? Was it Alissa Jordan?"

At the mention of Alissa's name, her mother's head snapped back to stare at Tara.

Her mother didn't need to say it. Tara could see it in her face. "Alissa sent you here? Why? How'd she find you?" The questions tangled in her throat and she couldn't say any more.

Her mother's face grew dark, her skinny lips biting off the words as she spoke. "Okay, yes. Some guy came around. Some snoopy little investigator guy. Said he'd been looking for me, had a job for me from some little snit named Alissa. She paid me to come here. All I had to do was get you away from this stinking horse show and I'd get a lot more."

She dropped the cigarette to the ground and stomped on it.

"You had to ruin it, though. You always ruin everything. You were always more trouble than you were worth. Just like that stupid horse—nothing but trouble."

Tara's mother tilted her chin higher, and hissed, "You didn't honestly think I'd want to keep you around did you? I don't want you. I needed the money."

Tara's lower lip quivered as her mother turned and stormed off across the parking lot. It had all been a cruel hoax. A hideous, evil trick.

"Look who I found," Sam called, strolling around the other side of the trailer. Cindy and Simone followed him. Tara's mother turned her head and stared back, the color draining from her face. In a rush, she darted through the maze of pickups and horse trailers.

Tara's legs trembled, giving way. She slipped to sit on the ground, tears gushing down her face.

"Tara!" Cindy raced up, kneeling down next to her. "What's

wrong? Are you okay?"

Tara continued to shake, unable to speak. She watched her mother fade in and out of the trailers, a horrible ghost from her past.

"Who was that?" Simone asked, staring after Tara's mother.

Tara bent over, wrapping her arms around her legs. Her stomach hurt. Her head hurt. Her heart hurt. "She," she croaked, "was my mom."

Silence overtook the small group as they all watched the woman continue to run, finally disappearing behind a large truck.

"She...was your mother?" Sam whispered.

Tara nodded, rocking back and forth.

"I'll be back," Sam muttered. "There's something I have to check out."

Cindy dropped next to Tara and wrapped her arms around her, caressing her face. Tara leaned in and rested her forehead against Cindy's shoulder, finding comfort and tenderness, the very things she had wanted from her mother's hug, now realizing were never there.

Sam stomped away. He seemed angry. At the moment she didn't care. She grabbed onto Cindy's arm and cried, "Why can't my mom love me? I wanted her to love me. She only wanted to get me away from Trouble." Tara hid her face in Cindy's shoulder, her body jolting with the sobs.

Simone knelt next to her and stroked her hair.

Tara didn't know how long they sat there. Five minutes, ten minutes...maybe longer. Finally she leaned back, her breath coming out in short quick bursts.

"I'm sorry," she said, blowing her nose in the tissue Simone offered her. "I guess you'd think I'd be used to this by now."

Cindy shook her head. "No, you don't have to be sorry. But I don't understand. What did you mean by your mother only wanted to get you away from Trouble?"

Tara bit her lip, forcing back a new wave of sobs. "Alissa paid her to come and get me out of here so I couldn't compete. I thought my mom really cared and came back for me. All she cared about was money. She was going to dump me all over again."

"That's terrible." Simone jumped up, her hands balling up into tight fists and staring off in the direction Tara's mother had disappeared.

The questions sloshed around in Tara's mind like leaves on an angry ocean. Her shoulders slumped. "Am I such a horrible person?"

Cindy helped Tara to her feet, brushing away the stray pieces of hay and grass.

"You are *not* horrible," Cindy said softly. "I know how much you wanted your mother to come back to you. This isn't your fault. You have to understand that. Some people aren't capable of loving."

Tara swallowed a sob. "But why? I'm her daughter. Why can't she love me? To her I'm just a major inconvenience."

Trouble reached forward and nosed Tara's arm, whickering softly. Cindy grinned. "I think Trouble disagrees."

Tara turned and wrapped her arms around Trouble's head. "At least Trouble is capable of loving me."

"Us, too," Simone said softly, looking slightly hurt.

Tara leaned back quickly, her eyes connecting with Simone's.

"We all love you, Tara." Cindy put her arms around Tara and Simone both. "We're here for you, whatever you need." She paused, searching Tara's face. "Do you want me to go scratch you from the race? I don't know how you can compete after this."

Cindy's words weighed heavy. Race? Scratch? She gazed back at Trouble. He was so trusting. So loyal. "No. We *have* to race." It started slowly, and quickly spread…conviction warming her insides, confident and strong. "I can't let Trouble down. Alissa's not going to win by cheating. We'll show her what we're made of."

CHAPTER TWENTY-FOUR

Tara straightened the cowboy hat on her head. It definitely fit different than the English helmet she'd worn her first day at Freedom Farms. She smiled, remembering the first time she'd met Cindy. Her life had sure changed since then.

Trouble nickered to a lanky Appaloosa. Tara recognized the mare from Freedom Farms, boarded six stalls down from Trouble. She'd remembered the Appaloosa's owner as a volunteer in the program and had seen her almost every day since summer started. Tara smiled and waved. "Hi, Laura."

Laura waved back, showing off the blue ribbon she'd received from the advanced Western pleasure class.

"Will you please hold still, Tara?" Cindy barked, a safety pin in her hand. "I don't want to poke you while I'm putting this number on the back of your shirt."

"Sorry." Tara forced her body to stand still. Her eyes still drifted across the fairgrounds surrounding them. "Where's Sam?"

Even more people flowed toward the arena, the time

growing closer for the racing events to start. The drone from the stands grew louder, anxious faces straining to watch the parade of horses starting toward the gate.

"I haven't seen him since he left," Simone said, searching the rush of people.

Cindy finished pinning the number, smoothing the paper. "He'll be here, don't worry. He wouldn't miss it for the world."

A dark car pulled up, parking next to the pick-up. Mr. McDonald got out and went to the opposite site of the car to open the door for his wife. Mrs. McDonald smiled and waved, a rosy glow filling her face. Though still a little weak, Tara thought she looked wonderful.

"We wanted to come and wish you luck," Mrs. McDonald said, patting Tara's hand.

Mr. McDonald gazed at Trouble and nodded approvingly. "You've made such a difference in that horse. He's really lucky you came along."

It was nice of them to say, Tara thought. "Thanks. But really, I'm the lucky one."

Mr. McDonald turned to Cindy, his eyes darting back to his wife. "I have something to ask you." His face flushed slightly. Was he nervous? Or excited? Tara wasn't sure.

Mrs. McDonald took her place at his side, grasping his hand, a sparkle flashing in her eyes. She pulled a photograph from her pocket with her free hand, the paper quivering. Their eyes connected, broad smiles spreading across their faces.

Cindy couldn't hide the question in her face. "What's going on, Dad?"

He cleared his throat. "I know you've been offered a training position with Scarborough Farms. However, I was wondering if we might interest you in a proposition at Freedom Farms instead."

"What do you mean?" Cindy asked, her brow creased with

question. "What kind of proposition?"

Tara was as confused as Cindy. Sam was their horse trainer at the farm. Was he leaving? Had he been keeping it from them? The thought terrified her. If he left, what would happen to Trouble?

Cindy caught her eye, and from her look, apparently wondered the same thing.

"It's a new position," Mr. McDonald rushed, obviously seeing their concern. "You see, Cindy, I have a young horse I've just acquired. She's a beaut. And she promises to be a good jumper. Has great bloodlines."

"You bought what?"

Mrs. McDonald nodded. "We want you to stay and train her…and, of course, show her. We've got several boarders lined up who want to learn to jump, as well as having their horses trained. We never realized there was so much interest. And Sam's too busy with all his other horse stuff. Doesn't care much for jumping anyway."

Cindy glanced from her dad to her mom and back.

"Of course, there is one catch." Mr. McDonald was trying to sound gruff, except Tara could hear the joy in his voice. "If you stay on, we want you to take some college business classes, too." He couldn't contain his delight any longer and smiled broadly. "We're not going to be able to run Freedom Farms forever, you know."

Cindy's eyes began to glisten. "But…but…are you sure?"

Mr. McDonald winked at his wife. "We've never been more sure of anything in our lives."

Mrs. McDonald held out the photograph in her hand. "And this is our new horse, the one we want you to train."

Cindy stared at the photo. Her hands began to shake as she pulled the photo close to her face. "She looks like Jupiter."

Mrs. McDonald nodded, her eyes radiating the joy in her

voice. "Her name is Jupiter's Dream Girl. She's Jupiter's granddaughter." She smiled coyly at Mr. McDonald. "Your father found her and has been working on her owner for over two weeks now. She'll be here the day after tomorrow."

Cindy stood speechless, one hand covering her mouth. A tear slipped down her face as she stared from the photo, to her parents, to Tara, and back to the photo. She reached out and hugged Tara tightly, then reached an arm up to include Mr. and Mrs. McDonald and Simone in a group hug.

After what seemed an hour of rapid-fire questions and answers between Cindy and her parents, Tara excused herself and made her way back to Trouble. It was happy news for Cindy. The kind of happiness Tara dreamed of. Home, family, love. Would she ever find that kind of joy? Could Cindy's staying mean happy news for her, too? Maybe Cindy would let her stay on at Freedom Farms now.

She knew the answer before she'd even finished her thought. Cindy would be really busy now. Too busy to worry about a foster kid. And Glenda was already working on trying to find another family. Tara would have to settle with seeing Cindy when she visited Trouble.

Mr. and Mrs. McDonald hugged Cindy one last time and waved good-bye.

"Good luck, dear," Mrs. McDonald called again to Tara. "We'll be watching in the stands."

"Yeah," Mr. McDonald added. "I'd say make us proud, except you've already have."

Tara waved, warm feelings rushing through her. She may not be able to live at Freedom Farms, but she would always be a part of it. A small taste of happiness—happiness none-the-less.

*****

The excitement of the crowd was contagious, voices talking all at once, rising to be heard over the next guy. Anticipation spilled over to the waiting horses and riders. Tara untied Trouble and walked him in a small circle behind the trailer. His feet danced in the dirt, his head and tail high. Tara placed a trembling hand on his neck, feeling the stares and glares of those watching Trouble, waiting for him to act up.

"You need to settle down and relax," she said softly, almost as much to herself as to Trouble.

Trouble nudged her playfully, rubbing his head on her shoulder.

"You better get checked in." Cindy pointed to a group of riders heading toward a man with a clipboard at the gate.

Tara pulled Trouble to her, feeling the need to be close to him for one last quiet moment. "You're the best horse here, Trouble. And we're going to prove it—to everyone."

Mechanically, she led Trouble across the fairground, turning back to wave to Cindy and Simone. They waved in return and headed to the stands. Watching them go, she realized they were on their own now. Her and Trouble. Surprisingly, she wasn't afraid. As she found Trouble's eye, she knew why.

After checking in, Tara mounted and rode Trouble into the holding pen where the riders were to wait. Alissa practiced along the opposite rail, galloping Solomon at full speed, jerking and spinning him in tight circles. Tara kept to her side, keeping her distance. She didn't need a confrontation with her. Not now.

Rider after rider entered the big arena, whooping and hollering, galloping around the barrels, some elated with their times, others angry with a tipped barrel adding precious seconds to their run. Tara watched and waited, her stomach tied in knots. Some riders started from the left side, some started from the right. It didn't matter. They just had to complete the cloverleaf pattern. The best time won. A young girl on a tall black horse knocked down two of the three barrels in her run. But instead of yelling or being mad at her horse, she praised him for finishing the race, patting his neck, smiling.

"That's a five-second penalty per barrel. It'll kill her time," the dark-haired girl next to her said. Her voice shook. Tara recognized the gray horse as Trouble's new friend at the neighboring trailer.

"She doesn't seem upset," Tara replied. "Hope I can be as good a sport if that happens to me."

The girl smiled, a look of pride growing in her eyes. "Yeah, she is a good sport, isn't she? She's my little sister. I guess she did pretty good for her first year." The girl nudged her gray forward. "Well, good luck. It's almost my turn."

"Thanks. Good luck to you, too."

The stands were filled to overflowing, people standing all around the steps and lining the railed arena. Tara searched the stands for a familiar face, finally finding Cindy and Simone halfway up on the right side. She waved and they waved back. Over from them, Janie watched the rider in the arena, her eyes following intently. Sam was still nowhere to be seen.

"I can't believe you're still here," Alissa's voice growled.

Tara turned and instinctively put a reassuring hand on Trouble's neck. Trouble snorted and danced to the side. The pen was mostly empty by now, those finished waiting in the opposite pen.

Alissa looked coyly around at the remaining riders, glancing to make sure they were all busy, too busy to pay attention to them. She leaned closer and glared at Tara. "Guess your stupid mom is as big a loser as you are. She couldn't even do one simple thing. It should've been so easy."

Tara swallowed, fighting the urge to snap back. She closed her eyes, hoping to follow Janie's advice and not be rattled by her, to let the comments slide off. It wasn't working. Her mother's face appeared in her thoughts, sneering, insistent, angry when she couldn't get Tara to leave Trouble. Tara gripped her stomach. Don't throw up. Don't throw up.

"Oh, what's the matter, Tara? Your momma dump you again?" Alissa's voice was cruel and sharp. "You're really stupid if you actually thought she came back for you. Why would anyone come back for *you*? No one cares about you, not unless there's cash in it for them."

Tara's eyes flew open. Enough! Anger burned like a hot poker. "That was a dirty, rotten thing to do, Alissa." She flexed her fingers, gripping the saddle horn tight. "How could you?"

Trouble pranced to the side beneath her and she could feel her own emotions ripple through him. She pulled on the reins and took a deep breath, trying to curb her rage. She couldn't let Trouble get upset and mess up everything they'd worked toward. Not because of her. Not because of Alissa.

"You are so thick," Alissa hissed. She jerked her reins and Solomon whirled around, his eyes rolling with confusion, worrying the bit in his mouth. "And, I'm not going to let someone like *you* make a fool out of me. You'll see."

"Make a fool of you? What have I ever done to you?" Tara couldn't believe her ears. "Why are you doing this to me?"

An evil smirk pulled Alissa's face to one side. "I do it because I can," she sneered. "You're so stupid. Why don't you give up and go home? There's no way you and Trouble are going to win today. You're both losers. So leave and save yourself the embarrassment. And believe me, I *will* make sure you're embarrassed." She flipped her long blonde braid and smacked Solomon in the rear with her whip. Solomon bolted forward with a frightened grunt.

Trouble snorted and pawed at the ground. Tara mutely laid a hand on his withers. Was Alissa right? Were they going to go out there and be the laughingstock of the horse show? This was all so new and she really didn't have a clue how to race.

Trouble turned his head, nibbling on the toe of her boot,

watching her with a trusting eye. Tara stared back. The image of the little girl on the black horse replayed in her head. It didn't matter how they scored. It only mattered that they tried.

She smiled, feeling the anger and despair flow out of her like a soothing rain. "Win or lose, Trouble, we're not going to let Alissa stop us. We're going to prove her wrong, about both of us."

Riders continued running, taking their turn, tearing around the arena. The announcer reported the times to the cheers of the crowd. Sixteen point seven… Seventeen point one… Sixteen point eight plus a five second penalty for a total of twenty-one point eight.

The girl on the gray horse rounded her last barrel and raced down the home stretch. Tara clapped her hands and cheered as she brought her horse across the finish line. "Sixteen even, our new leader," the announcer blared. The girl rode out of the arena, her face beaming, her sister giving her a high-five.

"You're next." The man with the clipboard pointed at Tara, then glanced up at Alissa. "You're on deck."

Tara's hands tingled as she sat deeper into the western saddle and readied her reins. She nudged Trouble into the arena and took one last glance to the stands. Mr. and Mrs. McDonald sat behind Cindy and Simone. And there was Sam, next to them. He nodded at her and gave her a thumbs up. Tara exhaled, relieved to see him there.

Trouble pranced in place, pulling at the reins, sending bolts of electricity shooting through Tara's arms. The gate man signaled the clock was ready. Tara leaned over and whispered into Trouble's black-tipped ears. "Come on, Trouble. Let's have some fun."

Giving him plenty of rein, they jetted across the starting line toward the barrels. Trouble shortened his stride, turning at Tara's command to round the first barrel. Tara grabbed onto the saddle horn and lowered her face closer to Trouble's neck. Now the second barrel. The wind stung her eyes and Trouble's black mane slapped at her cheeks. Still she kept her eye on the metal drum. She laid the reins on Trouble's neck again and they bent around the barrel, circling it ever so close.

"Come on, Trouble," Tara called. "You can do it."

Trouble galloped across the soft ground toward the third barrel. With a fraction of an inch to spare, he circled the final barrel and sprinted toward the finish line, flattening out, lengthening his stride.

"Fifteen point ten," the announcer shouted. "A new leader."

Tara's heart pounded as she pulled Trouble to an excited trot, patting his shoulder. "You did it, boy. You did it."

"Oh, save it," Alissa snapped as she pushed past the gate man before Tara could even get out the left gate. Solomon tossed his head up and down as she yanked his reins, white rings surrounding his dark eyes. "You can't beat me. I won't let you."

Tara ignored her tirade and directed Trouble into the opposite holding pen. It didn't matter what Alissa said anymore. It didn't matter if they won. None of it mattered. In her heart, Trouble had already won. He'd proven himself a champion, win or lose.

"Our final contestant," the announcer called. The gate-man started to nod the timer was ready. Before he could lower his head, Alissa jerked Solomon toward the barrels. Solomon reared and bolted forward. Alissa fell forward on his neck. Recovering, she stiffened in the saddle, face livid. Raising her whip, she whacked the horse's hips wickedly. Solomon weaved uncertainly toward the barrel. Alissa yanked the reins back and forth. Solomon struggled around the first barrel and headed toward the second, Alissa lashing him again and again, pressing him forward.

Solomon's eyes grew wilder by the second and grunted as he charged toward the third barrel. Alissa yanked the reins viciously, bending him toward the barrel...close, too close. Solomon's chest clipped the rim, knocking it over, the drum rolling in front of him. He tried to jump it but his front hooves smashed into the metal with a loud *clash*.

Tara watched, horrified, as the sorrel tumbled over the barrel, falling on his side with a heavy thud. Alissa jumped free, screeching with rage. Trouble jerked his head, sidling next to the metal gate.

As Solomon struggled to get his feet under him, Alissa jumped on his neck, beating at his head with the leather whip, smashing the riding crop down onto his ears and forehead. "You...let...her...beat...me!"

"No." Tara screamed, pressing Trouble into action, steering him toward the center of the ring. "Stop!"

CHAPTER TWENTY-FIVE

In one deft move, Tara pushed open the gate and pointed Trouble toward Solomon. Alissa raised her whip, crazed eyes locked on the fallen horse. Trouble burst past her and Tara seized the whip from Alissa's raised hands, the surprise knocking her backward off Solomon's neck. A low rumble sounded as Solomon rolled over and clumsily got to his feet. He shook his red mane, defiance blaring from his open mouth. He lunged toward Alissa and reared up, hooves pawing at the air.

Alissa raised her hands over her head as Solomon's sharp hooves sliced ever closer to her head. Tara reined Trouble toward Solomon again. Trouble laid his ears back, shoving his shoulder into Solomon's side, forcing him away from Alissa. Solomon dropped to the ground and stamped at the dirt, his eyes flashing. Tara grabbed his dangling reins, dragging him to the center of the arena, away from Alissa.

A safe distance away, she hopped off Trouble, her knees shaky and weak. Talking quietly to Solomon, she calmed him, soothing him. She was probably going to be in trouble for this, but she had to stop it.

Alissa put her arms down and stared after Tara. Solomon's reprisal seemed to be forgotten and her eyes darkened.

"What do you think you're doing with *my* horse?"

Solomon jerked back at the sound of her voice, his eyes rolling as he danced against the reins.

Alissa took a bold step toward Tara, stopped, and turned to gawk at the silent stands. The crowd stared back, spellbound. The color drained from Alissa's face, her eyes wide, mouth gaping.

A low murmur rolled through the crowd. One man stood up and made his way along the aisle, his stony face red and angry. Mr. Jordan.

He marched down the stairs and stood at the edge of the plowed arena, facing his daughter, exasperation in his stance.

Alissa straightened her shoulders, the color coming back to her face, the darkness returning to her eyes. "Did you see that?" she screamed at her father. "Tara has my horse. Aren't you going to do anything about it?"

Mr. Jordan raised himself up to his full height, rage building in his chest, his jaw twitching.

Alissa stared into the audience, searching the stunned faces. "It's all her fault." She pointed back to Tara. "She ruined everything." Her shoulders slumped slightly. She yelled again, this time with less conviction. "It's Tara. It's her fault."

Mr. Jordan took two steps into the plowed field and motioned to the spot in front of him. No words needed to be said. Alissa's face reddened and with one last glance at Tara, she slunk off to her father, empty-handed.

"And our winner is…" the announcer blared into the hushed arena, "number forty-four, Tara Cummings."

A thunderous cheer roared from the crowd. Tara stood in the center of the arena, Trouble on one side and Solomon on the other. The people in the stands rose to their feet, clapping and cheering. Tara could tell the praise was as much for her saving Solomon as for winning the race. Trouble and Solomon bobbed their heads with the excitement, swishing their tails, ears pricked sharply. Sam, Cindy, and Simone bounded down the steps and across the soft dirt to her. Sam nodded, his face alight with his smile and took both sets of reins from Tara.

"You did it, Tara," Simone squealed, jumping and dancing. "You did it!"

Tara shook her head, happy tears streaming down her face. "It was all Trouble. I just went along for the ride."

Cindy teared up and embraced her in a giant hug.

After a long squeeze, Tara reached back to hug Trouble, noticing a tear slipping down Sam's face as well. He was proud of her and Trouble, too. There was something else as well, though Tara couldn't quite put her finger on it.

The judges made their way to the middle of the arena and presented Tara with a large purple rosette ribbon, clipped to a golden trophy cup, a statuette of a horse and rider bending around a barrel attached to the front. Tara's hands trembled as she took the trophy and showed it to Trouble. "It's yours, boy." Happy tears flowed down her cheeks. "You're a champion."

"You're both champions," Sam said, his voice cracking.

* * * *

Back at the horse trailer, Tara stored Trouble's saddle into Sam's truck and grabbed a brush.

"Congratulations," the girl on the gray horse called.

"Thanks," Tara called back. "You, too."

Well-wishers had stopped her all the way back to the trailer and even now a steady stream of people filed by, shaking her hand, patting her back, and looking admiringly at Trouble. Tara couldn't hide her happiness. She was so proud of Trouble. She was proud of herself. They'd done it. They won. More importantly, they hadn't let Alissa stop them. She stopped in mid-brush and hugged Trouble's neck.

Sam set a fresh bucket of water down for Trouble, glancing at Tara, smiled, his eyes misting.

"Congratulations, Tara," a woman's voice said. Janie's mother, Georgia, stood at the edge of the pick-up. "Janie's really happy for you. You did a great job out there. It's remarkable what you've done with Trouble."

"Thanks. He *is* an amazing horse."

Georgia nodded. "Janie wanted to come tell you herself, but I made her go rest in the car. She is pretty upset at the moment." Her face grew serious and she looked at Sam. "I'm supposed to tell you…" She paused. "…we found out who threw the fireworks in the barn."

Tara gasped as Sam motioned an obviously shaken Georgia to a chair next to the truck.

She waved it off and continued, "Thomas Jordan was parked next to us. He and my husband have been friends for years. When I took Janie back to the car after the race we overheard Alissa…confessing…to the fireworks, to how she blackmailed Clancy, even how she stole money and jewelry from the other boarders at the farm in hopes of getting Tara kicked out.

"As you can imagine, Janie was livid, what with the fireworks and…" Georgia's voice faltered.

Sam shook his head. "Why did she go after Janie?"

Georgia looked to Trouble. "She wasn't after Janie. She thought Janie was Tara, taking Trouble back to his stall. She was after Tara and Trouble."

Tara swallowed. The movement next to the barn that day. It had been Alissa.

Georgia frowned. "Thomas asked me to tell you. He's selling all Alissa's horses. She's going to pay for the damage she caused. And he said he'll be calling you to set things right."

The pieces of the puzzle had all been put together. Still Tara was confused with the feelings running through her. She thought she'd feel happy once Alissa was punished. Instead, a twinge of sadness tugged at her.

"Well, thanks for letting us know," Sam said. "I'll wait for Mr. Jordan's call."

"Thanks Sam." Georgia looked back to the parking lot. "Well, I better get back to Janie." She turned and gave Tara a small smile. "She wanted you to know how happy she is for you. And how brave you were to save Solomon. "

"Tell her thanks, from both Trouble and me."

Georgia walked away, weaving through the horse trailers. Sam leaned against the end of the trailer and gazed at Tara. "Well, I guess the mystery is solved." He appeared anxious. "Are you doing okay? You've had an awful lot happen today as well."

Tara brushed Trouble's back. "I'm actually better than okay. I never thought I'd say this…but…I feel sorry for Alissa. She always tried to make my life miserable, and now I think she's more miserable than I've ever been."

Sam cleared his throat, watching her. What was that look in his eyes? Was he upset? Sad? Afraid?

He took a breath. "You proved everyone wrong. We'd all given up on Trouble. If it hadn't been for you, the Jordans' would have had him destroyed."

"I couldn't give up on him."

"I know." He gazed at Cindy and Simone, sitting in lawn chairs beside the pick-up, inspecting the trophy. He turned back to Tara. "A lot of people gave up on you as well, didn't they?"

The past seemed like ancient history. She toyed with the memories, thinking half out loud. "Yeah. I guess so. I guess I had given up, too. Coming to Freedom Farms and meeting Trouble changed all that. I know I can deal with almost anything, or anyone, now. I have friends, people who care. And I have

Trouble."

Sam nodded and cleared his throat again. It was beginning to make Tara nervous.

"Would you like to stay at Freedom Farms?" Sam began. His voice was low, hesitant.

Tara eyes brightened and she searched Sam's face. "Really? Do you think I can? Will I stay with Cindy? Has she said something?" She glanced quickly at Cindy, then back to Sam.

Cindy, noticing Tara's excitement, got up and joined her and Sam. Simone followed her.

Sam looked down at the ground. "Tara, I've been so blind." He flexed his hands as if trying to pump up his courage. "Some people never learn to love. It took me a long time to accept it. Some people love too much. And some people don't even know they're loved."

What was he saying? "I don't understand."

Sam looked back up. "Tara, your mother is the woman who destroyed my world. She's the one who left me."

Tara gasped. Her mind whirled. Sam? Her mother?

Sam rushed on, not letting her dwell on her thoughts. "I loved her so much and I was devastated when she left. It took a long time for me to quit blaming myself. But it wasn't me. She didn't know how to love me. She never will. After talking to her today, I understand now."

Tara's eyes misted. She remembered his voice the night he'd talked about her. It must have been really hard for him to see her, let alone talk to her. "I'm sorry if she brought all that pain up again."

Sam put a hand on Tara's shoulder. "No, I'm glad she came back. I mean…I'm not glad, ah…I mean…" He shook his head, seemingly disgusted with himself. "Seeing her again made me understand…it's not my fault."

Tara tilted her head. "Of course it's not your fault. She left you. She left *me*." Tara stopped, his meaning coming into focus. It wasn't her fault either her mother had left. She hadn't done anything wrong.

"Seeing your mother also brought certain things to light I never knew existed." Sam swallowed. "Tara...I just found out...I'm your..." He cleared his throat again. "...you're my daughter."

Tara stepped back, her heart hammering in her chest. "You? You're my father?" The words of her mother echoed in her head. "She said you left. You chose horses over me." She wasn't sure how she was supposed to feel.

Sam stood tall, his eyes pleading. "No, Tara. Never! I didn't know about you. She disappeared and I never saw her again. I didn't even know she was pregnant. Tara, I would *never* have chosen *anything* over you."

Silence overcame the group as Tara let the truth sink in. She thought of all the days at Freedom Farms, how she admired Sam, thought of him as a father-figure. How he'd talked about the woman he loved leaving him, tearing his world apart. How he'd wanted a family. She was his family. "You're really my dad?"

Cindy reached up to smooth Tara's hair. "Sam told us when he got to the stands." Her eyes searched Tara's face. "Do you know what this means?"

Tara's face broke into a giant smile. "It means I not only have wonderful friends...I have a family. A real family!" She leaned forward and fell into Sam's open arms. Happy tears flowed down her face. Trouble nickered and bobbed his head.

* * *

Tara leaned against Trouble's shoulder and took a deep breath, smelling the wonderful earthy smells of the farm. The sun sparkled off the barn's new coat of whitewash, and a new sign stood at the highway announcing Cindy as new co-owner. Trouble tugged at the lead, munching happily at the bounty of grass under his feet. Cindy led Dream Girl to the arena and after inspecting the jumping saddle, mounted and rode her in a wide circle around the pattern of fences and small blocks. Tara smiled. Dream Girl was beautiful, her dark hide glistened, muscles rippling as she loped around the arena. Her long mane was braided neatly, making her neck look long and elegant. She gave a playful buck and tossed her head. Cindy reined her toward the first jump and crouched forward in the saddle, hands steady. Tara's heart soared as the mare sailed over the hurdle, inches to spare.

Trouble raised his head, his eyes following Cindy and her mare, a low whicker rumbling his content.

Cindy's small house had received a new coat of paint as well and Tara could see the familiar curtains in her old bedroom and thought back to the many nights she'd sat by the window, wondering how she could survive away from Freedom Farms. She smiled. She wouldn't have to find out now.

Mr. McDonald ambled out of his house on the hill, arm in arm with Mrs. McDonald, and headed to the rose garden. Her health was returning since her heart attack and she couldn't resist the urge to tend her flowers. Mr. McDonald insisted on going with her to do all the lifting and pulling.

Sam led a long-legged palomino filly from the barn to the pasture gate across the driveway. He patted the golden neck and let her go, a deep laugh sounding on the breeze as she ran off, bucking and whinnying to greet and play with the other yearlings.

Trouble nudged Tara's foot, trying to get her to move aside, green stems sticking out the sides of his mouth. She laughed and stepped aside, allowing him full access to the clover.

"If this is all a dream, I hope I don't ever wake up."

She stroked Trouble's face and gazed at the activity of the farm.

"I have a new home...a dad who loves me...good friends

who care about me. And in three weeks, I'm headed to Maxwell High, the same high school as Simone."

Trouble snorted and raised his head. Tara stared into his large brown eyes, eyeing the reflection of a content and confident teenager.

"Most of all, though, I have you."

She glanced up. Sam waved at her from the door of the barn. She waved back, the warmth of her new home filling her.

"We won't ever have to leave Freedom Farms. We belong here."

ABOUT THE AUTHOR

C.K. Volnek spent far too many nights dreaming of horses. In grade school she read every horse story she could find and still begged her parents for more. She'll never forget her 12th Christmas when she received her first real pony, a beautiful Welsh-Arab cross named Sunny. And so her love for horses grew through the years; riding, showing, and spending time with the many horses she loved. There is something truly magical in the bond of a girl and her horse, a special kind of love that will never die.

C.K. Volnek also authored "Ghost Dog of Roanoke Island," which was released in September, 2011.

Made in the USA
Lexington, KY
24 March 2014